DEAD OF NIGHT

A BURKE AND BLADE MYSTERY THRILLER
BOOK 5

MICHAEL LISTER

This is a work of fiction. Names, characters, business, events and incidents are the products of the author's imagination. Any resemblance to actual persons, living or dead, or actual events is purely coincidental.

For Vanessa
In appreciation for the journey and the work.

THE BURKE AND BLADE SERIES

Read the entire Burke and Blade Series.

Lucas Burke and Alix "Blade" Baker are Panama City Beach PIs specializing in missing persons cases--work they were led to by their own sister's disappearance.

Growing up in foster care and children's homes has made them tough, savvy, and streetwise, but nothing has prepared them for this.

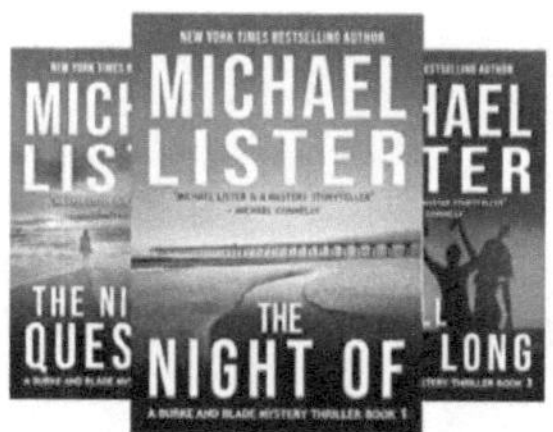

CHAPTER ONE

"YOU BETTER HANDLE THIS ONE," I say.

Blade glances over at me. "For real? Figured you'd be all over shit like this."

"I'm legit scared I'll kill him."

"Yeah, and?" she says with a smile.

We're entering Oaks by the Bay park at the end of Beck on foot. It's late-thirty on a school night in early November and the park is dark and mostly empty.

Oaks by the Bay is an urban green space next to the shoreline of St. Andrews Bay in the revitalized historic waterfront village of St. Andrews. Its ancient, spreading oaks and tall, thick-bodied pines tower over the paved walking paths, gazebo, park benches, and boardwalk, and obscure the bay beyond.

Only the occasional movement of a dark figure in the darkness or a barely audible conversation shatters the stillness and quiet.

We're here for Chad Meeks, who is here playing Pokémon Go, the augmented reality mobile game that uses mobile devices with GPS to locate, capture, train, and battle virtual creatures known as Pokémon.

He's a seventeen-year-old white boy, tall and thin with coarse brown hair that sticks up like he just got out of bed.

We've been following him for the past couple of hours, hoping his hunt would lead him to a secluded location. Now we're hoping it will take him to the back of the park.

"Look like ol' Chad is finally cooperatin'," Blade says.

"Finally," I say.

I don't like being away from Ashlynn and Alana this long—especially at night.

As Chad passes under Old Century, the massive oak believed to be over 350 years old at the center of the park, he pockets his phone for the first time tonight and picks up his pace.

"Shit," Blade says, "his ass must'a caught 'em all."

We increase our speed and begin to narrow the gap between us as Chad enters the canopied boardwalk that leads through the pines down to St Andrews Bay.

When he reaches the observation platform at the water's edge, he quickly takes the steps to the right down to the small sandy beach.

We take the ramp to the left and come up behind him as he's peeing in the sea oats on a small dune.

"So," Blade says, "wasn't Pokémon but a call of nature that brought you back here."

He jerks his head around to look at us, while his body remains facing forward in the peeing position.

"The fuck, bruh. Give me some privacy."

"Interstin' you should say that," Blade says. "Privacy is what we're here about."

"Huh?"

He's clearly confused, as yet unaware of his precarious predicament.

I step behind him, bring my arms up under his and around his neck, putting him into a full nelson.

As I spin him around, Blade steps forward with one of her

knives but quickly stops and jumps back as a string of pee slings out toward her as if from a sprinkler.

"Your ass lucky that didn't get on me," she says.

I'm not sure if she's talking to him or me until she adds, "I'd'a killed your skinny white ass on principle alone." At which point I'm reasonably certain she's talking to him.

"What the fuck?" Chad says.

"Oh, wait," she says. "Ah, shit. Our bad. We thought you were a Pokémon. We thought we'd finally captured the elusive Charidouche."

"*What*?" Chad asks, even more confused now.

He tries to wiggle out of my hold, but he is a weak, skinny adolescent and it doesn't take him long to realize it.

"Chad," Blade says, "I got to tell you. It's for . . . It's fortu—" She looks at me. "What word am I tryin' to say?"

"Fortuitous," I say.

She looks back at him. "It's fortuitous that we found you with your pants down like this."

"*Huh*?"

"You know what fortuitous means?" she asks.

"Huh?"

With her right hand still holding the knife close to Chad, she uses her left to remove her phone from her pocket. "Hey, Siri," she says, "tell Chad what fortuitous means."

Siri offers to text a contact in her phone named Chad the statement "Tell Chad what fortuitous means."

"Send?" Siri asks.

"No, don't send that shit," she says. "Hey Siri, what does fortuitous mean?"

"Fortuitous," the feminine robotic voice says, "happening by accident or chance rather than design."

"Did you hear that, Chad?" she asks.

"Huh?"

"Chad, your vocabulary seems pretty damn limited. I'm just

tryin' to help you out. But you know what they say. You can lead a douche to a dictionary, but . . ."

"Hey," Chad says, "aren't y'all the ones who found that missing girl?"

"We are," Blade says. "And we're here tonight to see if we can find your missin' humanity."

"My wha . . ."

With her phone still out, she lowers it and takes a few pics of Chad's small, flaccid dick.

The flash is brilliant against the darkness and I'm blinded for a few moments. When I can see again, I mostly see spots.

"The fuck you doin'?" Chad asks, some defiance back in his voice.

"Violating your privacy," she says. "While contemplating violating you in other ways."

She takes a step back and snaps a few more pics. These more full-frame images capture both Chad's face and Little Chad in the same photo and I'm blinded all over again.

"Little warning would be nice," I say.

"Oh, like you gave me when you slung the pee at me?"

"I didn't sling it *at* you," I say. "But point taken."

"Chad," she says, as she steps back closer to him and brings the knife back to his pale, boyish face.

"Huh?"

"We're here for Harley," she says.

He shakes his head. "She's not here."

Blade laughs. "Oh, no, that's not what I meant. That's funny. No, I didn't mean for her as in we're here to get her. I meant for her as in on her behalf."

"We work for her," I say. "She hired us to hurt you, but we're seriously considerin' killing you for no additional fee."

Blade says, "Harley told us somethin' very distressin' about you, Chad. She said when she broke up with you, you told her you'd taken nude pics and videos of her having sex with you without her knowing and that if she tried to leave you you were going to share them with . . . what was the phrase . . . her 'friends, family and the whole fuckin' world.'"

Chad's body goes as limp as his dick.

"You know what that's called, Chad?" she says. "That's called revenge porn. And it's got to be one of the most wicked, vicious, and douchey things a little douche like yourself can do."

She pauses for a moment and lets that hang there in the darkness between us.

"It makes me want to kill you with my bare hands," I say, my mouth right at his ear. "It's why she's the one dealin' with you. I have anger issues and I'm afraid if I started hitting you I wouldn't stop until you were dead and your face was unrecognizable.

"Now, Chad," Blade says, "I'm gonna ask you a question, and I want you to think long and hard before you answer it and I want you to tell me the absolute truth. I want you to tell me the truth like you know if you don't I'm literally going to cut your little dick off, okay?"

He nods and lets out a jagged, crying, "*Okay*."

"Have you shared or shown any pics or videos of Harley to anyone?"

"No," he says. "No. I swear."

"Swear on your dick?" Blade says.

"I swear to God."

"Not the same thing," she says. "But okay. Are the pics and videos anywhere besides on your phone?"

"No. I swear."

"Not even backed up to the cloud?"

"I . . . I don't have a cloud."

She reaches over and withdraws his phone out of his pocket.

"What's your passcode?" she asks.

He gives it to her.

She enters it. And in another moment she's in his phone.

"Okay, Chad," she says, "here's what's gonna happen. We're gonna take your phone. Our forensics experts are gonna see if you lied to us. They'll be able to tell if you sent it to anyone. If you haven't—"

"I haven't. I swear."

"We'll soon find out. Meantime, don't say a word to anyone. Understand? Not to anyone. If you say anything or if we find out you been sharing or postin' any of the pics or videos of her . . . it's gonna cost you your dick. That's why I took a picture of it. I'm gonna show it to everybody before I cut it off. Understand?"

"I haven't shared anything with anybody. I swear."

"If you're tellin' the truth, then we'll wipe your phone and get it back to you."

"And we'll be watchin' you from now on," I say. "If you ever do anything like this again—or mistreat a young woman in any way we'll come back and extinguish your flame. You won't even know we're there. We won't say anything. It'll just be . . . lights out. Tell me you understand."

He nods.

"Tell me," I say.

"I understand. But I swear I was never gonna do it. I was just tryin' to get her not to break up with me."

"Chad, I gotta say," Blade says, "that's not the best way I've heard of to make your ex think she made a mistake in breaking things off with you."

I say, "What we do is who we are. Is this who you are, Chad? This who you want to be? A creep? Someone who exploits and terrorizes young woman?"

"No," he says. "That's not me."

"That is you," I say. "That is exactly who you are. But it's not who you have to be. You get to decide who're you going to be moving forward. Understand?"

"Yes, sir."

"Every choice matters," I say. "Every decision. Every single one."

"I'm sorry," he says. "I'm so sorry."

"If that's true," I say. "You just might have a chance."

CHAPTER TWO

BY THE TIME I get back to my place, Alana is asleep.

It's the biggest disappointment of my day. I was hoping to see her before she drifted off—maybe even play pretend or some of the games she loves so much.

Since she and her mom moved back to Panama City they've been living with me.

We're sharing a small, one-bedroom apartment in St. Andrews, she and her mom using my bedroom and me taking the couch. Because of Dimitri Sokolov's threats against them, Blade, Bobby Doll, Pistol Pete, Clyde Broussard, and Lexi Miller are helping me provide round-the-clock protection, which means there's always someone else here as well. That's a minimum of four people twenty-four hours a day. I'm an introvert with a need for time alone, something I'm not getting right now. But it's a small price to pay to keep them safe.

Tonight Pistol Pete is here.

He's sitting at the small kitchen table reading a textbook on homicide investigation. He's wearing a shoulder holster with a Glock in it and a 12 gauge shotgun is on the table not far from his phone.

Pistol Pete Anderson is not only our brother from the foster program, which makes him Alana's uncle, but he's also an investigator with the Bay County Sheriff's Office and a hell of a shot. He's lean, clean-cut, in his late twenties, and has pale skin and short reddish-blond hair.

"How was the night?" I ask.

I whisper it because Ashlynn is asleep on the couch.

"Uneventful," he says. "Just the way we like it. How'd it go with revenge porn guy?"

I nod. "Good, I think. We'll see."

Unable to help myself I say, "I'm gonna go look in on her. Be right back."

"Since you're here, I'm gonna step outside a minute."

I quietly enter my room through the slightly open door and make my way over to the bed.

I love watching Alana sleep. I love the way she always sleeps at a diagonal angle and takes up far more space on the bed that her small frame should be able to. I love the rhythmic pattern of her breathing. I love how calm and peaceful she appears. When awake she is rarely still, so the best and clearest looks I ever get of her are from pictures or when she's sleeping.

Though she is the daughter of my foster sister, Ashlynn, I feel like she's my own.

I love Alana in a way that I was never loved when I was her age. Or any age. I adore her with something so pure I've never experienced it before.

I've never had a family. Not really. What I have with certain of my fellow fosters is as close to family as I've ever come. And Alana is the center of that family. She's its heart, its breath, its vitality.

Her innocence and wildness, her joy and kindness touch me in a place I didn't know I had. And her fragility and vulnerability cause me to wake up nights in a cold sweat.

I'm not sure how much longer we can live like this, not sure how much longer I can allow Dimitri Sokolov to live.

Ashlynn stumbles into the room and eases into bed.

"Night," she says.

"Sleep good," I say.

I turn and take a few steps toward the door.

"Sorry about all this," she says.

"You have nothing to be sorry for," I say. "I'm the one who brought the Russian mob into our lives. Besides, I love havin' y'all here. You know that."

When I walk back into the main room, Pete is coming through the door with a heavily inked dark-haired pixie.

She's wearing a paint-spattered sheer slip dress, bright red high heels, and stylish black-rimmed glasses. Her short, thick dark hair is coarse and curly and has bright floral hairpins nested in it. Beneath her thick dark brows her black eyes, magnified by her glasses, appear intense and intelligent and maybe a little mad.

"Found her lurking in the parking lot," Pete says. "She's not armed."

"I wasn't lurking," she says to me. "I was tryin' to decide if I was going to bother you at home or wait until you were in your office. I've been by a few times lately and can never catch y'all there."

"We've been busy," I say. "Not really takin' on new cases right now."

"I'm a true crime junkie," she says. "Followed y'all for a while now. Read everything. Listened to the podcasts. I'm sure y'all get all the work you want, but I'm beggin' you to hear me out. A horrible injustice has been done and I have no one else to turn to."

CHAPTER THREE

HER NAME IS LUNA COIL. She's an art student at Gulf Coast State College. And she believes her stepmom was murdered.

She is seated on my couch, her blag bag, which is on the floor next to her, has a spiral-bound sketchbook sticking out of the top of it. I'm in the armchair next to the couch. And Pete is back at his chair at the kitchen table.

Her slip dress reveals pale skin, large, natural breasts, and elaborate tattooing. Her right arm has a full, colorful sleeve. Her left is covered with random designs.

"I was pretty horrible to her," she is saying, "but that's not why I'm—I feel guilty, but that has nothing to do with the fact that she was murdered and it's been covered up."

Her voice is soft and airy and sounds like she's trying very hard to shed her southern accent.

Pete says, "What's your stepmom's name?"

"Tracy. Tracy Adams."

"I remember that case," he says. "Out at the beach, right?"

"It was an adult slumber party," Luna says. "A birthday party for Adeline Ashby. It was at her house. It was supposed to be just women, but the husband and a friend of his crashed.

Tracy was the only black woman there and the only one not in any of the friend circles and the only one not wealthy. And the only one to wind up dead."

I vaguely remember the case. Seems like it was determined to be an accidental death.

"I wish she'd've never gone to that stupid party, but she was so like honored they invited her. They had never invited her to do anything before. If they didn't invite her for the express purpose of killing her, they must have invited her to clean up for them."

"Are you sayin' she had no connection to any of the people at the party?" I ask.

"She had some loose connections. She had cleaning company and she worked for a couple of them. She went to high school with a couple of others. And they all had sons in an AAU basketball league—I guess that's the sort of umbrella connection this particular group had. My stepbrother Jamal was the only one of them with real talent, the only one who didn't have to buy his way on the team. They were all jealous of him."

"I know you're sad and upset," I say, "and I'm not tryin' to diminish your loss, but . . . the kinds of things you're sayin' don't usually lead to murder."

"I'm not sad or upset," she says. "I didn't like Tracy. My dad is upset. Her children are upset. Her friends are upset. I'm not. I told you . . . I'm not doing this because I liked her or miss her or feel guilty. I'm askin' for your help because I don't want those rich bitches to get away with it. They always get away with everything. There's different rules for them. I'm sick of it."

Luna has a large mouth full of big, bright white teeth, and her lips are thick with bright red lipstick. When she's not speaking her mouth remains closed and still, her face expressionless.

"It was ruled an accident, right?" I say. "What makes you think it wasn't?"

Pete says, "And that was after a lengthy and thorough investigation."

"I don't have a smokin' gun or anything," she says, "but I'm also not just sayin' it's a feeling I have. The evidence is there. You just have to look at it. That's all I'm asking y'all to do. Look at the case."

"I'm definitely going to look at it," I say, "but like I said we're not really taking on new cases right now. We've got—"

"Just look at the case," she says. "That's all I'm asking. See if you see what I do. If you do and want to do something about it that'd be great. If you don't, then I'll take it to someone else. But . . . I know y'all are right for this case. I know y'all can get justice for my family."

CHAPTER FOUR

"WE SAID WE NOT TAKIN' any new cases right now," Blade says.

It's the next morning and we're in our office.

"I know."

"Thought we gonna finally find Kaylee," she says, referring to our foster sister who went missing when she was in college and we were kids.

"We were, but . . . I was thinking . . . we can't leave town until we solve our Dimitri problem."

"Only one way to solve that."

She thinks we've got to kill him and she's probably right. I just keep hoping someone else will do it or he'll move back to Russia.

"So, since we can't leave town . . . why not take a look at Tracy Adams' case?"

"We can leave town," she says. "Just have to take Ashlynn and Alana with us."

"And the four people helpin' us guard her?"

She shrugs and frowns, the closest she's going to come to conceding the point.

"Will you just hear what they have to say?" I ask.

Luna and her dad are on the way to our office.

"I'll hear what they have to say," she says, "but I ain't gonna be easy to convince."

"Wouldn't have you any other way."

A few minutes later, Luna appears in our doorway, her dad just behind her.

She is wearing a pair of navy canvas painter pants and a thin wife beater, both of which are spattered with paint. Today, instead of a handbag, she has a small forest-green backpack, but like the handbag, it also has sketchbooks poking out of the top.

"Come in," I say.

They slowly ease into the office.

"It's not easy for us to be in here," Luna says. "This firm represented the lead investigator in Tracy's case. Y'all don't work for them, do you?"

"From time to time," I say. "Like any other client."

"We independent AF," Blade says.

"This is my father, Nate Adams," Luna says.

Nate is a mid-forties white man with closely-cropped blond hair, striking green eyes, and a deep tan. He's shortish and carries some extra weight, but his arms and chest are large and hard. Dark shades dangle from a bright aqua rubber string around his neck and there are pale lines from them on his sun-reddened face. He's wearing khaki shorts, laced work boots, and a white short-sleeved sports shirt that has Nates Landscaping Services printed on the upper left corner.

"Nice to meet you, Nate," I say. "Y'all have a seat."

Nate nods but doesn't say anything. He looks a little lost, like he's just following Luna's lead.

They ease down into our client chairs like they're still not sure they should be here.

"What did Lewinsky, Clemons, Bradley, and Sykes represent the lead investigator in the case for?" I ask.

"He was involved in all sorts of unethical and illegal activities—and not just in Tracy's case," Luna says. "He was suspended over shit he did in Tracy's case and ultimately fired. These creeps tried to get him his job back."

Nate says, "Fact that they failed makes me think there may be some justice in the world."

"You say that, but you've given up on getting any for Tracy," Luna says.

"Yeah, I guess I have." He looks at me and then Blade. "Truth is, Luna's the only one who hasn't given up."

"And I'm not goin' to—not until those spoiled rich fucks pay for what they did."

"And what is it you think they did?" Blade asks.

"Killed Tracy."

"All of them? Together? In some sort of conspiracy?"

"I don't know. I don't know who actually did it. That's what I want y'all to find out. I know y'all specialize in missing persons cases, but Tracy is missing. She's missing from our lives. Missing at the table at holidays. Missing from my dad and her son's lives."

"If we take the case," Blade says, "we'll do a deep dive and find out everything we can, but can you just give us an overview?"

"Adult slumber party for Adeline Ashby's birthday at her house. Thirteen women, including Tracy and Adeline. Her husband, Steve, and his friend, Ryan Bowman were not supposed to be there, then they were just going to stay down in the game room away from the women, but eventually came up stairs and joined the party. The eight women had various connections but Tracy wasn't close with any of them."

"She wanted to be," Nate says.

"She was the only black woman there," Luna continues. "The only one not in any of the friend circles. And the only one to wind up dead."

"How did she die?"

"They say from an accidental fall off the balcony," she says. "According to the people at the party she stayed up later than everyone else. Went out on the balcony to smoke and was so drunk or high or whatever she went over the railing. She was found facedown, flat on the ground in a spot not possible to land in if you fell off the balcony."

Nate says, "The balcony was only on the second floor. That's only twenty feet or so. Twenty five if you count from the top of the railing. A fall from that height doesn't kill anyone, does it?"

Luna says, "Of course, it doesn't. And her injuries weren't consistent with a fall. I won't go into them now because it would take too long, but there's no way to sustain the injuries she did from falling off a second story balcony onto the ground."

"What else?" Blade asks.

"The investigation was a joke. It was treated as an accident from the very beginning. No rape kit. No real interrogations. Very few pics. No crime scene processing. Wait 'til you hear the 911 call. Adeline and Steve told the police from the beginning that it was an accident and the cops just went with that."

Nate adds, "They didn't even turn her over or try CPR. They kept sayin' she was stiff but they also claimed not to have touched her. They were not her friends. But she wanted so badly to fit in with them. I begged her not to go. Then I begged her to come home with me. But she wouldn't listen. I wish I'd've insisted."

"Not all the women stayed the entire night," Luna says. "Two had to get home to relieve babysitters. They're husbands picked them up around midnight. Dad tried to get Tracy to do that."

"I could tell by her voice and her texts that she was drinking a lot and maybe even on something else too."

"Which the autopsy later confirmed," Luna adds.

"One of the times we were talkin'," Nate says, "she just put the phone down. One of the other women picked it up and said they thought I should come get her. So I tried, but she wound't leave. If she would have she'd still be alive now. I got such a bad feeling when I was there. I should've—"

"You did everything you could," Luna says. "You're not to

blame." She looks back at us. "That was around midnight. Around one most everyone went off to bed. Only Tracy and one other lady stayed up. A woman named Brandy. In her statement she says she and Tracy were eating gumbo and drinking and talking. She says around two-thirty she decided to go home. She had planned to stay the night but changed her mind. She said when she left, Tracy said she was going out on the balcony to have one more smoke and then she was going to bed. At six the next morning one of the women got up to go to work and saw Tracy facedown on the ground. She woke up Adeline and Steve and who knows what happened after that, but whatever it was . . . it took a while 'cause they didn't call the cops 'til almost eight."

"You mentioned the investigators not doing a rape kit," I say. "Do you think she was raped?"

"We'll never know," Luna says. "But . . . it's a hell of a motive for murder. And it's not hard to see one or both of the men lifting Tracy over the railing to throw her off the balcony. Not sure any of the skinny white bitches that were there could've done that."

"Okay," Blade says. "We're not taking on any new cases right now, but . . . let us talk about it and see if there's anything we can do. We'll get back with you soon."

"That's all we can ask," Nate says. "We appreciate your time."

"Just take a look at the autopsy report," Luna says. "If that doesn't convince you nothing will."

CHAPTER FIVE

"WHATTA YOU THINK?" I ask.

Blade shrugs. "I'm intrigued."

Luna and Nate are gone and we are alone in our office.

"Want to look at a few things and talk to Ben before we take it on, but I'm leanin' toward a *yes*."

"She's right about the autopsy report," I say. "Her injuries don't seem consistent with a second story fall to the ground."

"You've read it?"

"Just skimmed it."

"But whether she fell accidentally or was pushed, she died from the fall, right?"

I shrug. "Throwin' her off the balcony could've been to conceal injuries she already had."

She nods slowly, seeming to consider that.

"The other things is the position of the body," I say. "She was facedown on the ground, completely straight and flat, like she face planted. Hard to see someone falling from twenty or twenty-five feet and landing like that. And the body is too far away from the balcony. Looks like it would've taken a running jump to get where she landed—and I'm not sure that would've done it."

As I'm talkin', she flips through the file Luna left with us. "Blood alcohol level has her drunk as fuck," she says. "Also had weed and Xanax."

"Everyone says she brought the weed," I say, "but she didn't take Xanax and didn't bring any to the party. The one woman who did have a prescription for Xanax swears she didn't share any with anybody."

"'Course she does."

"She was pretty fucked up," I say. "Which is why the cops concluded she went off the balcony on her own. Theorize she either lost her balance—which is hard to see how that gets her over a four-foot rail—or she leaned over the railing to throw up and somehow fell over. But if that's the case . . . how does she land face down with her arms down at her sides and so far away."

She nods as she continues flipping through the file.

"The house had an elaborate security system," I say. "There's a record of every time a door is opened or closed. There were cameras, including on the balcony, but they weren't charged and didn't capture anything."

"Convenient."

"Yeah."

"This says there were reports of arguing and fighting between the women that night," she says, "and even the men got involved at some point, but there's nothing like that in the police report."

"Not much of anything in the police report," I say. "Even if it was some kind of bizarre accident . . . it was a half-assed investigation. The police were also called out earlier that night because the neighbors complained of noise—and not just music but yelling and screaming. This report doesn't even mention that one."

"The fuck?" She says, shaking her head as she looks up from the file. "Steve Ashby worked in the state attorney's office."

"Yeah. He knew the cops conducting the investigation," I say.

"Told them it was an accidental death on the 911 call before they even got there. Directed them the whole way. He was reprimanded for using his position to access the case info while the investigation was happening."

"Corrupt fuck," she says. "Oh, we takin' this case. Even if it was an accident, I want these fucks to be give an account."

CHAPTER SIX

"WHAT OUR CLIENT may or may not have done doesn't change the fact that the poor woman died as the result of an accidental fall," Ben is saying.

Ben Simmons grew up in the system with us and is one of our brothers. He's an attorney here at Lewinsky, Clemons, Bradley, and Sykes and the reason we have an office in their building.

He's a thin, smallish late-twenties man with dark, stylishly short hair with a boyish face and a bit of an undeveloped appearance, and he's sitting in our client chair where Nate Adams had been about an hour ago.

"Cut the lawyer bullshit and tell us the real deal," Blade says.

"That is the real deal. What Mike Reeves did had no bearing on the investigation."

"What exactly did he do?" I ask.

"Well, what he lost his job over was having affairs with multiple women. Often while on duty. Often with women involved in his cases—victims, suspects, witnesses. And he talked to them about his open and ongoing investigations."

Blades says, "He fuck around with any of the women at the slumber party?"

"At least one that we know of," he says. "Tara Barnes.

"And you don't think it has a bearing on the case?" she says.

"I don't think it changes it from an accident to a homicide."

We are all silent a moment.

"Think about some of the shit you two get up to," he says. "Not all of it legal or ethical, is it? But it doesn't change the facts of the cases you work or whether they're accident, suicide, or homicide."

"Don't know who you been talkin' to," Blade says, "but we *never* do anything illegal or unethical."

"And let me say," Ben says. "Off the record, of course. Mike Reeves is a racist, misogynist piece of shit. He's a bad person and a bad cop. But that doesn't change the facts of the case."

"What racist shit did he do?" Blade asks.

"What racists shit didn't he do. He referred to the case as the uncoordinated porch monkey case. He wrote a pretend email he never sent to Nate Adams. Pictures surfaced of him in blackface at a party."

"What'd the email say?" I ask.

"Something like Hello from Racist Cracker Copland. I'm writing to tell you that your uncoordinated porch monkey of a missus is dead as hell and not coming back. Good luck raising your little porch monkeys. Tell them not to do drugs and get fall-down drunk like mama monkey."

"Fuck," I say.

"I know," Ben says. "Nothing we could do to save his job."

"Good," Blade says.

"But get this," Ben says. "He just ran for sheriff in a little county not far from here and he won."

"'Course he did," Blade says.

"There were other people connected to the case who did similar stupid shit, but it doesn't change what happened."

"Like who?"

"Like Steve Ashby," he says. "The birthday girl's husband. He worked in the state attorney's office and accessed the case files during the investigation. Not sure if he did more—like try to influence the investigation, but—"

"There's no doubt he did," I say. "He did from the very first moments of the 911 call."

"Or," Ben says, "he's just describing what he sees and stating what he thinks is obvious."

"How 'bout we listen to the 911 call?" Blade says.

"I've heard it too many times to count," Ben says, getting up. "I'll leave it with you. Let me know if you need anything else from me."

CHAPTER SEVEN

911 OPERATOR: 911. What's the nature of your emergency?

Adeline Ashby: Hi, yes, I need an ambulance and the police at my house 544 Sand Dune Court.

911 Operator: Okay. What is your name?

Adeline Ashby: Adeline Ashby.

911 Operator: Okay. What's going on?

Adeline Ashby: We had people over last night and one of them stayed up smoking on the balcony, and when we woke up this morning, we found her face down on the ground and she's stiff. She was drinking. It looks like I'm guessing maybe she fell off the balcony.

911 Operator: Okay. Is she breathing?

Adeline Ashby: I don't think so. She's stiff.

911 Operator: How old is she?

Adeline Ashby: 41 . . . I think. Here, hold on.

Steve Ashby: Hello, this is Steve Ashby.

911 Operator: Have y'all checked to see if she's breathing?

Steve Ashby: She's face down on the ground . . . not moving. Not breathing. She's stiff. I've tried to assess the . . . her, but . . . she's completely facedown in the backyard and not . . . She's stiff.

911 Operator: Okay. If she's not breathing and you know she's gone just leave her where she's at. Do you see any blood or anything? Are you there? Do you see any blood or anything from where she fell?

Steve Ashby: I don't know. I . . . don't know if I should move her over or leave her where she is. There's some blood on her wrist I think. Her hands are down by her sides. All we can see is her back.

911 Operator: Do you know if she's . . . if she was suicidal at all?

Steve Ashby: I have no clue. I've only met her one other time. Like my wife said she came over last night for her birthday party —not the woman who we believe to be deceased, but my wife's birthday party. It was a group of friends that came over. They decided to stay in instead of go out. They were drinking and hanging out. She was the only one smoking. She would go out to the balcony to smoke throughout the night. She drank a lot. More than anyone else. She was the last one up when everybody else went to bed. She was either waiting around for a ride or waiting 'til morning. She must've gone back out for one more smoke before bed and somehow fell off.

911 Operator: Are there security cameras?

Steve Ashby: Oh, yes. There are. There are. I forgot about . . . There are.

911 Operator: How far is where she would've fallen from? How far is the deck from the ground?

Steve Ashby: It's probably 20 feet . . . if she was . . . from where her feet would've been on the railing.

911 Operator: So you think she climbed up on the railing?

Steve Ashby: No. I don't know. I just meant. I don't know what I meant. I was just trying to describe the . . .

911 Operator: And what is her name?

Steve Ashby: Tracy, maybe. I think . . . Hold on a moment. Her name is Tracy Adams.

911 Operator: Was she there with anyone else?

Steve Ashby: Do you mean at the party or on the balcony?

911 Operator: Either.

Steve Ashby: I don't think so. I think she came alone. I think she . . . She was the only one smoking. I thinks she came out for one more smoke before bed. I'm on the . . . I'm out on the back deck right now and I see cigarettes and a lighter and an empty bottle of rum. She was the only one drinking that.

911 Operator: Okay. Are all the people who were there last night still at your house?

Steve Ashby: Hold on. It looks like four have already left.

911 Operator: Okay. And they just left this morning or they left last night?

Steve Ashby: Some of both, I think. We can check. We have an alarm system. There will be a log of every time the exterior doors opened and closed. I think the last time I saw Tracy was about one in the morning before I went to bed. She was in the kitchen. About to head back out to the balcony.

911 Operator: Okay. I have the . . . A deputy is pulling into your driveway.

"They started peddlin' it as an accident from the jump," Blade says.

I nod. "Certainly did."

"And what was up with how calm they all were?" she says.

"Most sedate 911 call in history," I say. "Even when Adeline passed the phone to Steve . . . she didn't seem too upset to talk."

"Somthin' off about the whole thing."

I start to say something, but she reacts to something in the file.

"Hold the fuckin' phone," she says. "Did you look at the guest list?"

"I did."

"Why didn't you tell me your girlfriend was there?" she says.

"I don't have a girlfriend."

"Oh, my bad. Why didn't you tell me *one* of your *girlfriends* was there? What was she doing there?"

"A," I say, "I don't have a girlfriend or girlfriends. And B . . . I'm havin' lunch with her today to find out."

CHAPTER EIGHT

HEATHER HARRISON IS or was a poet. Her daughter, Leah, went missing from their condo on the beach during a hurricane and was never seen again. Blade and I worked the case and found out what happened to Leah. Since then, Heather and I had been seeing each other—only occasionally and only casually—and it's not only because I'm also seeing Lexi Miller, my probation officer, and Heather is nearly old enough to be my mother.

We meet at Thai Basil near the end of Beck Avenue in St. Andrews. She is sitting at a booth in the back when I walk in.

I see her before she sees me.

She is so slight, so petite, that the booth seems to swallow her up.

She's not on her phone. She's not people-watching. She's just sitting there, calm, composed, self-contained.

I am drawn to her in a way I am no one else on the planet. Blade is convinced it's maternal and has to do with my mommy issues. And that may be part of it, but if it is, it's a small part. I think it has far more to do with how broken she is—and the fact that it's not self-inflicted brokenness. I know far more damaged people—people who regularly take a blowtorch to their lives, people who pile on what life has done to them by abusing drugs and alcohol and other self-destructive behaviors. That's not Heather. She sits with her damage. She befriends it. She neither ignores or compounds it.

The worst thing that can happen to anyone happened to Heather. In losing Leah she lost everything—eventually including her entire family. She is broken beyond repair, damaged down to her DNA. Her wounds are fatal but she hasn't succumbed to them yet.

She stands when she sees me and we embrace.

"Sorry I'm late," I say.

"You're not."

She has saved me the backside of the booth so I can keep an eye on the doors and I slide into it.

"It's so good to see your sweet face," she says.

We haven't seen much of each other lately. I've only been back in town a short while and guarding Alana and Ashlynn from Dimitri leaves little time for little else.

"It's great to see you," I say. "Sorry I haven't been very available lately."

She looks better each time I see her, as if now that she knows what happened to her daughter there's a certain slight cellular reanimation taking place. Her once flawless forty-something-year-old face still appears to have been carved by grief, but her skin is not as paper-thin as it has been.

"I'm also sorry this has to include questions about a case," I add.

"Don't be," she says. "I'm happy to help try to get some justice for Tracy."

"That mean you don't think it was an accident?"

She shrugs and shakes her head. "I don't know . . . but I do feel like there's a lot that didn't come out."

A stocky young man in black with a white apron comes over and takes our order. She gets panang curry and I get red curry. With both get a level four spicy.

"How are you?" she asks when the waiter leaves the table.

"I'm okay. Happy to have Alana and Ashlynn back. But . . . I worry we won't be able to protect them."

"You will."

"How have you been?" I ask. "You look like you're . . ."

"Less of a walking corpse?" she offers. "I am. Thanks to you and your partner. I'm probably about as good as I'll ever be able to get. Certainly far better than I ever thought I would. I . . . I'm living a sort of half-life and that's about half more than I thought I ever would."

"I can tell you from experience that half-life is better than no-life."

"It certainly is."

We fall silent a moment, each taking a sip of our drinks.

"I worry about you," she says.

"Don't waste your time doing that," I say.

"Y'all do so much good, but it's so dangerous."

Before I can respond, the waiter brings our soup and spring rolls.

"Are you still seeing Lexi?" she asks.

It's the first time she's ever asked me so directly.

"I haven't been able to see anyone," I say. "I'd like to see you once we solve our Dimitri problem."

"I'd like that. I've been doing the online dating thing but it's pretty damn brutal out there."

I nod and smile and say, "I bet," but I'm filled with a sense of isolation, loneliness, and jealousy. We've only seen each other a little and we've never been exclusive. She knows I see Lexi some too. And since she's old enough to be my mom I've never believed we could have anything other than what we do, but thinking about her going out with other men and presumably looking for a relationship makes me sad.

"It's good that you're getting out there," I say.

What did I think—that she'd continue to not have a life and only see me when it was convenient for me?

"It's not good for my self-esteem, but it is, I guess, another sign of life."

I nod. "Can you tell me about the night Tracy Adams died?"

"Sure," she says, "that's why we're here. Are you okay?"

"Whatta you mean?"

"I don't know. You seem to change."

"Sorry for the abrupt transition," I say. "I need to get back to check on Alana and Ashlynn."

"Oh. Okay. No problem. Well, I was never part of their group. I didn't know them very well. I'd say I was even more of an outsider than Tracy was. She worked for a few of them. Went to high school with some of them. Kyle was attempting to play basketball. And I was attempting to be supportive. I was trying to give him a life. It was disastrous. I was sad and awkward and tryin' to pretend I cared about any of it. When Adeline invited me, Kyle begged me to go. I thought it was the least I could do. I was such a shit mother. So I went. I made up an excuse about not being able to spend the night or even stay long."

"What time did you get there?" I ask. "What time did you leave?"

"Got there around seven . . . Left around eleven. Tracy was the last one to arrive. She got there around eight-thirty. So I was only there a couple of hours while she was, but . . . it was enough."

"Enough?"

"Enough to see how she acted and how they treated her."

"And how was that?"

"She acted nervous and uncomfortable, but she overcompensated by being the life of the party. It was like she was performing for an audience. It was way too much. Being loud and jumping into every conversation. Trying to make them laugh. And she was throwing back drinks like . . . She brought a bottle of rum for Adeline, but Adeline said she didn't drink rum, so Tracy opened it and began to drink it. As far as I know she was the only one to drink any of it and even before the time I left, half the bottle was gone."

"And how did they treat her?"

"Like . . . Like a novelty. You know the way white people who aren't around black people very often act—like that. They definitely looked down on her. They found her entertaining, but they were mostly laughing at not with her. Some of them treated her like the help, asking her to do certain things they wouldn't ask anyone else to do. *Tracy, would you grab that for me? Tracy, could you put this up for me? Tracy, could you take care of this?"*

Our food arrives and we begin to eat.

"Are you sure you're okay?" she asks.

I nod. "Sorry, if I'm distracted. Got a lot goin' on."

"I know you do and I understand. It's not that. It's that you seem to change."

"Sorry. No, all good. I'll try to act better."

"I'm not asking you to act any certain way. Just want to make sure you're okay."

"I am. Thanks. Would you say Tracy was drinking more than everyone else?"

"No. Definitely not. Or if she did, it was only slightly more. I didn't drink much, but everyone else was tossin' 'em back."

"A lot of the witness statements indicate she was drinking a lot more than anyone else."

"They would say that, wouldn't they?"

"What about drugs?"

She shakes her head. "Nothing overt or out in the open," she says. "Adeline's husband worked in the state attorney's office and she told us ahead of time they couldn't have any drugs in the house. But I saw a few things being passed around. Pills mostly. But a little weed too."

"The reports—again, based on the witness statements—indicate Tracy was the only smoker and the only one going out on the balcony throughout the night to smoke."

She shakes her head. "I don't even think she was a smoker. I think she said she like havin' an occasional cigarette when she drank, but I think it was mostly weed she was smoking out there. And she certainly wasn't the only one. Several of the women were vaping. They were passing around an e-cigarette with pot in it and I'm pretty sure it wasn't Tracy's."

"Did you see her go out on the balcony while you were there?"

She nods. "Yeah. A few times. But I can tell you this. She never went out there alone."

"Do you remember who went with her?"

"No. Sorry. Like I said I didn't know these women very well at all."

"The autopsy showed Xanax in her system, but she didn't have a prescription for it."

"A woman named Jamie I think was passing them around."

"Jamie Hodgins," I say.

"Yeah."

"She swears she didn't give anyone any of her Xanax."

"She didn't . . . give any one. She gave everyone who wanted one."

The waiter comes and clears away our dishes and leaves the check.

"Let me get this," she says.

"Absolutely not," I say, as withdraw my company credit card and drop it on the small silver tray. "You're doin' me a huge favor. Besides, it's deductible."

"Well, thank you. It was delicious."

"Just a couple more questions before we go," I say.

"Of course."

"Did Tracy argue or fight or have conflict with anyone?"

"Not so much overtly, though she did seem to grasp pretty early on that they were laughing at her and not with her, that a lot of what they were saying and doing was at her expense. But there was this tension just under the surface of . . . everything. I didn't notice it until she got there. I'm not sure what it was about but it seemed centered on Tracy. It's hard to describe but it was . . . palpable. It didn't involve everyone, but . . . it involved several people."

"Can you remember who it did involve?"

"Adeline and her husband. His friend. Brandy. Tara. Jamie. A woman named Cher or Cherry. There may have been more. That's all I can remember for sure. There was a woman who seemed as uncomfortable about it as I was and who went out of her way to be kind to Tracy. I think her name was Natasha."

"And finally your opinion," I say. "Was Tracy's death an accident like the cops concluded?"

She shakes her head. "No. No way. Absolutely not."

CHAPTER NINE

NATASHA LEONE OWNS and operates a coffee truck called Mug Shot. Today it is parked in a lot on 4th Street next to the Center for the Arts.

The old box truck has been painted black and has white lettering and an order window in the side. The logo on the side of the truck and on every cup is an actual mug shot of a younger Natasha.

"People think it's Photoshopped or something," she says. "But it's the genuine article. I was involved in protest that got out of hand in my younger days."

She's an early-forties white woman with a massive amount of thick, wavy, unruly blond hair, big brown eyes, and a low, scratchy voice like someone went at her vocal cords with coarse sandpaper.

"Cool. Your whole set up has a nice vibe."

"Thanks. I'm here 'cause one of my girls is sick. We'll have to talk in between customers."

"No problem. I appreciate you makin' the time for me."

"I feel so bad for what happened. I keep wondering if I could've done something differently to have prevented it."

"Have you come up with anything?"

"I should've stuck closer to Tracy," she says. "I wish I hadn't gone to bed when I did. If I had stayed up with her, had her sleep in my room . . . I don't know . . . maybe things would've been different."

"Did you have any reason to believe she was in danger?"

"No. Not really. But you get that many mean girls in one place and . . ."

"Is there a core group that are friends?"

"Maybe, I guess. More like frenemies. And then there's the rest of us who are on the periphery. Not even sure why they keep us around—except to gloat about how good they've got it, compare their lives to ours. Tracy had started her own business like me. She was so proud of herself and how it was going. Some of the other women in the group own their own businesses, but they are million dollar businesses that they're families set them up in. So it's not the same. Not even close. We're like we own our own businesses too and they're like that's cute."

A customer approaches and she says, "'Scuse me a minute."

She enters the door in the back of the truck and is at the window by the time the customer is.

The customer is a tall, late-twenties woman with extremely large breasts and extremely thick black hair—and a lot of it.

"What can I get you?" she asks.

"I'll take an Airtight Alibi," she says. "At large and on the loose."

"You got it. Seven-fifty."

The young woman pulls out a credit card.

"Stick it right in there and follow the prompts on the screen. I'll have it right up."

While Natasha makes the coffee, I look at the menu. All the drinks are named after law enforcement terms to go with the Mug Shots theme. An Airtight Alibi is a sugar-free frappé with unsweetened oat milk. At large is a large size and on the loose means no whip cream. There is also the BOLO, the Perp, the Physical Evidence, the Under Oath, the Citizens Arrest, the 911, the B&E, the High-Speed Pursuit, the Body Cam, and many others. There's even a Misdemeanors menu for kids or adults new to coffee.

When the customer is gone, Natasha rejoins me near the rear of the truck.

She's carrying a coffee which she hands to me. "I made you a Detective First Grade."

"Thank you very much," I say.

Though Mug Shot's cups are plastic they are made to look like white ceramic coffee cups.

"This is fantastic," I say. "Thank you so much."

"Glad you like it."

"In the statements most of the women at the party gave they make it sound like Tracy was the only one drinking a lot, smokin', and taking pills."

"They're lying," she says. "Everyone drank. Some a lot more than others, but everyone drank. I'd say at least half were smokin' and at least a couple were poppin' pills."

"Was Tracy visibly wasted?" I ask. "Slurring her words. Unsteady on her feet?"

"If so, only by the end, but even then it seemed mild. I say the end, but it wasn't the very end. I mean by the time I went to bed."

"What time was that?"

"'Round one-thirty, I think."

"Throughout the night was Tracy outpacing everyone else?"

She shakes her head and her mass of thick blond hair waves about. "No. Absolutely not. She was more demonstrative—a mother who didn't get to go out much or party much there to have a good time, but there was a core group drinkin' just as much. Then there were a few who had to work the next day or had to relieve the babysitter later that night. They didn't drink nearly as much, but they all drank too. I can't tell you exactly who did the pills and pot because it was a little more on the down low. Had to make sure Steve could have plausible deniability or somethin'. But there was plenty of it going on. A big part of the reason the party was a slumber party at Adeline's was so they could get fucked up safely."

"Didn't turn out to be all that safely," I say.

"No, it didn't, and it cuts me up more than I can tell you."

"Did Tracy get into it with anyone? Were there any arguments or—"

"Nothin' ever got out of hand," she says. "Never came to blows or anything. But there was tension every time the AAU team came up. Tracy's son was a superstar. Some of the other moms resented that. One especially. A woman named Tabitha I think. Her son lost his starting spot to Jamal. Then he got suspended from the team over some infraction. I can't remember what, but it was obvious Tabitha thought Jamal's the one who told on him. I don't think that's the kind of shit you kill someone over, but . . . who knows these days. The only other thing I noticed was . . . at some point cops and guns and use of force and kneeling during the national anthem came up. Tracy and I were in the minority during that discussion. One of the women went on a pretty racist rant. Tracy was visibly upset. We both were. We tried to say a few things but they shut us down. Tracy left the room. Went out onto the balcony. I followed. Adeline told everyone to change the subject and not come back to it."

"What about the men?" I ask. "I understand they weren't supposed to be there. And then they were going to stay downstairs in the game room, but eventually came up and joined the party."

"Yeah, that was weird. It was just Steve and a friend of his named Ryan, but they shouldn't have been there. We were told it was going to be just girls. I mean, we're all in our pajamas and drinking and . . . Originally, Adeline said Steve didn't feel like going out so he was just going to stay down in the game room watching football. She never even mentioned Ryan. Maybe she didn't know about him. They came up at halftime of their game to get snacks and then they just stayed. I mean like fully joined the party. It was bizarre. And I'm gonna tell you. Something ain't right with Ryan. He was very aggressive. And he kept hitting on us. It was extremely uncomfortable. Steve and Adeline kept making excuses for him, saying he's just drunk. He's harmless. But he didn't seem harmless. Not at all."

"Did he hit on Tracy?"

"He was the worst with her. He was different. Showed even less respect for her. More aggressive, more . . . I don't know. It was bad. Made me very uncomfortable. I started staying close to her and told him to fuck off. I could tell he was pretending to be more drunk that he was."

"Anything else happen that night that—"

"This probably has nothing to do with Tracy or what happened to her, but Steve and Adeline got into a big fight. It didn't make sense and you could tell it was about stuff from before that night and they went into the other room so we didn't hear much of it. But it was bad. They're divorced now. Did you know that? They stayed together through the investigation and all that, but as soon as it was ruled an accidental death they split up. And it surprised no one."

"Do you think Tracy's death was an accident?"

She shrugs. "It could've been. But gun to my head . . . I'd say she was murdered."

CHAPTER TEN

I MEET Clyde Broussard in McKenzie Park in downtown Panama City.

We most often meet in public but secluded places where we can't be seen and heard.

The fountains are off and the homeless have been run out. The park is quiet and most of the benches are empty. Overhead the huge limbs of the towering oaks spread out and provide a canopy for the park below. The Spanish moss draping the branches gently waves in the bay breeze and birdsong can be heard though few birds can be seen. Their sweet songs join the desultory sounds of slow-moving traffic on Harrison and the actions, activities, and exchanges of humans doing business in downtown.

Clyde Broussard is an enormous black man with plenty of girth and muscle. Everything about him is solid and hard and dark. We have to each walk along the edge of the cement walkway in order to be beside each other.

Clyde, who has become an unlikely ally, works for Logan Owens the predator I put in the hospital—an act I went to prison for.

Since, ironically, Owens is considered my victim, and because one of the conditions of my probation is to have no contact with him, Clyde often serves as the go-between.

If I am caught violating any of the conditions of my probation I'll be sent back to prison to serve out the remaining two years of my sentence—or longer if additional charges are applied. As fucked up as it is, I work for Owens from time to time because he has video evidence that would both send me back and add time to my sentence and he's blackmailing me with it.

"Logan discovered something while he was on safari," Clyde says.

"Oh, yeah. What's that?"

"The dancer at Cloud Nine . . . Destiny. She's the one."

"God have mercy on her."

"Says he missed her so much he couldn't concentrate on bagging his big game and no workin' girl in South Africa could hold a candle to her."

I shake my head.

"He brought some big ass blood diamond and is having it made into a ring, but before he pops the question he wants you to take a look at her again and make sure she's true to him and he wants me to take the Russian off the board."

He had me investigate Destiny before. Within a few minutes of being in the VIP room of Cloud Nine with her she was giving me the same girlfriend experience she gives him. It's what she does with many of her customers or clients or whatever they are. I reported back to him through Clyde that she wasn't having an affair, which was true, but I didn't bother to tell him any of the other. I didn't want her getting hurt and I had, wrongly now it seems, assumed he'd soon move on to a newer shinier iteration of the fantasy.

"Says he wants your assurances she's really true blue and if he gets those and he moves forward and she's not then he'll turn over his evidence and put you back inside."

"And if I say she's not true blue?"

"Then he'll make her wish she was never born."

"You gonna let that happen?" I ask.

"No, but . . . all that means is he'll fire me and find someone who will let him do it—or do it for him. Same as with the Dimitri. If I try to take him out and fail or if I refuse to do it . . . he'll just find someone else."

"He's giving each of us our own Catch-22."

"I know what you're sayin'," he says. "Know what that means, but . . . what does it really mean? Where's it come from?"

"A Joseph Heller book that came out in the early sixties. It's a no-win situation that the creators of which use arbitrary rules and conditions to hide their abuse of power. It was just a matter of time 'til someone like Owens came up with something like this."

"What do we do?"

"You have more options than I do," I say. "What will he do if you quit?"

"Not sure. Might try to have my replacement take me out. May just wish me well. Hard to say."

"Maybe someone else will take Dimitri out," I say. "Or he'll have to run back to Russia."

"Both are possible. He's got a small army around him, so he'll be hard to get out from the outside, but Lev's still got loyalists. If they find out Dimitri took him out they might eighty-six his ass."

"He's a fuckup," I say. "Eventually, he'll fuck up. But . . ."

"Can we survive and keep that little girl safe 'til he does," he says.

"Can't help protect her if I'm dead or in prison."

He nods and then with a wry smile says, "Any books out there about how to get your ass out of a catch-22?"

CHAPTER ELEVEN

"HOW YOU GONNA PROTECT her from inside prison?" Blade asks, nodding toward Alana.

We are at the Floriopolis art center on Beck across from the Panama City Publishing Museum. The door is open and we are standing near the front with a view of anyone approaching.

Floriopolis Art Center is known as St. Andrews' Arts & Culture Metropolis. It's a narrow storefront in the heart of the historic area undergoing a renaissance. It not only exhibits the works of local artists but has ongoing drop-in and create art projects like the one Alana is working on now.

She is in a tall chair at a high table near the front, intensely focused on her own unique creative process.

When we walked in she had said, "I'm gonna need construction paper, glue, tape, scissors, and markers," but she continued to add elements, including a tin box of buttons, a glass jar of glitter, and a plastic bucket of lime-green slime.

"Obviously I can't," I say.

"So now we got to protect Ashlynn and Alana and our damn selves from Dimitri, deal with and do work for creepy Logan Owens, find out who killed Tracy Adams, *and* keep your ass from going back to prison."

"I mean . . ." I say with a small tilt of my head and a shrug. Then in my best cockney, "Idle hands is the Devil's workshop, don't you fink?"

It's mid-afternoon on a clear, coolish early November day. The traffic on Beck is light and St. Andrews is mostly empty and quiet.

The space Floriopolis occupies is so long and narrow it's like an exaggerated old shotgun house. When we had come in, we had quickly and discretely searched the place and checked to make sure the backdoor was locked.

Similar to a tiny home, every nook and cranny of Floriopolis is utilized for storage and/or to display art. The current exhibit is a mixed media show that combines drawings and paintings with cross-stitch in cool and funky ways.

"For real though," she says. "This the way it gonna be with Owens for the next two years?"

"Not necessarily," I say. "There's a chance he could repent of his sins and be born again."

"So what we gonna do?" she says.

"All the above," I say. "Everything on your list—and then some."

"You got more confidence in our abilities than I do and time management and survival skills than I do."

"If we have other options I'd be happy to hear them."

"I keep tellin' you," she says. "Shoot Dimitri and Logan in their fuckin' faces will solve a lot of problems."

"And create new ones," I said. "But . . . I'm not rulin' that out anymore."

"*Really*?" she asks, the pitch of her voice and her eyebrows rising.

"It's not about us," I say, then nod toward Alana. "It's about keepin' her safe. I'll only do it as a last resort, but . . . if it's the only way to protect her . . ."

"May just be."

One of the Floriopolis volunteers brings yet another jar of materials to Alana's table.

Alana looks up and says, "*Yes,*" as if whatever is in the jar was what she most needed at that moment to complete her masterpiece.

I look back at Blade. "Obviously, we'll try to take him out if he makes a run at us," I say. "But if I get violated back to prison . . . I'll do it on my way back in."

"That's all good and fine—unless we get rubbed out before then. At a certain point we gonna have to be proactive with this shit. Take the fight to them while we still able."

"I know."

"How much longer can we guard them 'round the clock?"

I nod. "Let's keep it up a little longer. I'll start the investigation for Owens to buy some time."

"We on borrowed time already," she says. "And our asses too broke to buy any."

I nod.

Alana turns toward us. I look to make sure she's okay.

"No peeking 'til I'm done," she says.

"I was just checking on you," I say. "I didn't look at your work."

"I don't want you to see it until it's done."

"I won't," I say.

"*I won't either,*" Blade says in an exaggerated voice.

She's not as close to Alana and often points out how Alana mostly ignores her. But Blade is a lot and she does not spend much time interacting with Alana, she probably frightens her a bit.

"I got hold of the tech who installed the security system in the Ashby's house," Blade says. "He's willing to meet with us."

"Cool."

"And I think we may be able to get into the house and take a look around."

"Really? How?"

"They got the big bitch for sale."

"Sweet," I say.

We could pose as potential buyers and do a walkthrough with a realtor , but we have a realtor friend who will help us and we won't have to pretend and we can take our time.

"Need to do it sooner rather than later," she says. "They got that shit priced to sell fast."

"We could—" I stop as I see a young Russian man approaching the building. "Take Alana to the back. Lock yourselves in the bathroom and call Pete and Bobby."

CHAPTER TWELVE

THE SHORT, young man has broad shoulders and well-developed muscles.

Beneath a bald head, he has a sloping forehead, blondish eyebrows, blue-gray eyes, a snub, slightly upturned nose, and a cruel mouth with a cleft palate scar bifurcating his upper lip.

He's wearing gray jogging pants, a white wife beater, a black hoody, and bright white and red Jordans.

He stops about fifteen feet from the door and raises his hands.

He then unzips his hoody and holds it open to show he has no shoulder holster.

Bending down, he raises both pant legs to show he has no ankle holster.

Finally, he turns around and lifts up his hoody in the back to show he has no weapon concealed at the small of his back.

He slowly turns back around and lifts his hands again.

"I'm unarmed," he says. "Just want a quick word."

He has no discernible accent.

I look back to make sure Blade and Alana are safely locked in the restroom, then step through the door and walk over to meet him.

"The enemy of my enemy is my friend," he says.

"That's what I hear."

"Lev was my uncle," he says. "Dimitri is my cousin. If he killed Lev he is my enemy."

I nod, unsure what to say to that.

"I have a proposal for you."

"I'm already seein' someone," I say. "Actually, sort of two someones."

"I hire you," he says. "You find out if Dimitri killed Lev. If he did, I kill Dimitri, which is how I pay your fee."

"We trade in US currency only," I say. "No chickens or wives or dead guys."

"It would solve your Dimitri problem," he says.

"Like I said, that's not how we do business," I say, "but if it were, we couldn't investigate Dimitri or Lev's death if we wanted to. Couldn't get close enough. No access. No one would talk to us. You need someone on the inside."

"Sure," he says, "but if I approach the wrong someone . . . it's lights out Losif."

"Yeah, it's a real pickle," I say. "Well, good luck."

I turn to head back inside.

"Wait," he says.

I stop and turn back toward him.

"Tell your cop friends . . . I am willing to wear a wire. Bring down Dimitri another way."

"I'll pass it on," I say.

"He has to pay for killing Lev."

"You don't know that he did," I say.

"He did it. I have no proof. But I know he did it."

"If you're going to kill him if he did it and you know he did it . . ."

"I need proof for the family or . . . I take Dimitri out they take me out."

"Got to think they won't look too favorably on wearing a wire no matter what Dimitri did."

"Special dispensation if Dimitri popped Lev. Lev was loved."

Pete screeches to a halt on Beck, his emergency lights flashing, and jumps out, gun drawn.

"On the ground," he yells. "Hands out where I can see them."

Losif slowly does as he's told.

"Says he's not armed," I say. "Also says he wants to talk to you about wearing a wire ."

"Hands behind your back," he says.

Losif complies and Pete cuffs him.

"You wanna talk wires," he says. "Come with me and I'll hear you out."

He pulls Losif to his feet and pats him down. "Let's go."

"Thanks, Pete."

"I'll holla at you later," he says.

"Later," I say.

CHAPTER THIRTEEN

JAMIE HODGINS LIVES in a three-story beach house on the Gulf side of Highway 98, just down from Pier Park on the west end of Panama City Beach.

The multi-million dollar mansion is only one of the homes she and her property developer husband own.

I park my humble black Ford Escape between the Land Rover and Lexus in the driveway and we get out.

Lexi is with me. We're posing as podcasters working on Tracy's case.

Dressed in our hippest clothes and accessories we look the part of creatives with a vision.

The bead bracelets around my wrists, which match the necklace dangling around my neck and mostly open shirt, shake as I knock on the door.

Jamie opens the door right away, as if she was standing there waiting for us to knock.

"Come in. Come in. Welcome."

She's a forty-something with wispy bottle-blond hair who has had far too much plastic surgery. The filler in her face has her so plumped out she looks like she's having an allergic reaction.

"I'm Jamie," she says, extending a manicured hand with long, red nails and lots of diamond rings.

"Spike," I say, shaking her hand. "And this is Willow."

She and Lexi shake hands.

"Come through to the back deck," she says. "I thought we could have cocktails and watch the sunset while we talk."

"Cool," I say.

The wooden deck is wide and extends into the small remaining dunes. There's a full bar, a fountain, and several fire pits around which are exterior chairs and couches.

"Pick your poison," she says, nodding toward the bar. And would you be a dear and make me a vodka martini."

I jump behind the bar and mix a couple of low-alcohol drinks for me and Lexi and a very strong vodka martini for Jamie.

Lexi wanders over to the railing and gazes out at the view.

A few moments later, Jamie and I join her.

Handing them their drinks, I say, "Cheers."

"Cheers," Lexi says.

"Mazel tov," Jamie says.

We clink our glasses and then turn our attention westward.

The sand looks like sugar, the Gulf like melted emerald, and beyond sand and sea the fiery orange orb slowly descends.

It's hard to say what witnessing something so beautiful and powerful in such a peaceful environment does for the soul, probably because it's ineffable, but it's palpable, and I try to widen my eyes and breathe more deeply to take it in.

Eventually, I close my eyes to hear what the view is making me deaf to.

Suddenly, the wind whipping around me sounds like it's dancing and the slow, rolling, relentless tide comes to the fore of my focus as the waves gently slap and splash the shore.

"Let's have a seat and talk true crime," Jamie says.

Her words are intrusive and instantly take me out of my moment of peace and calm.

She walks over and reclines on a chaise lounge near a fire pit.

We follow and take seats in standard chairs across from her, the orange-blue gas flame dancing between us.

"So," she says, "pitch me."

"As you know there's nothing more popular than true crime podcasts and documentaries," I say. "We've made several successful ones and the one thing we know for sure is you have to have a hook. The hook for the one we're working on now is when someone dies as the result of an accident or suicide and his or her family and friends and the online true crime community try to make it out to be murder."

She nods vigorously. "Oooh, yeah. I like that. Do you know we actually receive death threats from those crazies? It's unreal how obsessed people become and how they can't let it go and believe the authorities who said plain as day this was an accident. You know?"

"Oh, we know," Lexi says. "It happens far more than you'd think. Loved ones want someone to blame."

"Yeah, me. It's so unfair."

"Exactly," I say. "And no one is telling your story."

"They most certainly are not."

"That's where we come in," Lexi says.

"Well, come on in," Jamie says.

"Our new show is called Victims of Accident," I say. "And it's focused on the true victims of cases like this—you and those like you."

"It's so true," she says. "We really are. Don't get me wrong . . . I realize the, ah . . . Tracy was a victim too. But she was a victim of her own ill-advised decisions. What happened to her was . . . self-inflicted, but the rest of us . . . we're innocent victims. Simply wrong place wrong time, innocent bystanders. I'm so glad someone is finally seein' this."

"We do," I say.

Lexi adds, "We see you. And your friends and the thousands of other innocent victims in similar scenarios."

"Well, sign me up," she says. "I can't speak for the others, but I'm on board."

"Excellent," Lexi says.

"There's not a lot of money upfront," I say, "but when the royalties kick in—"

"I look like I need money?" she asks, with an expansive gesture pointing out the beachside mansion we're currently sitting in.

"No, ma'am, you don't," Lexi says, "but there will be money. Just not a lot up front."

Jamie looks at me and holds out her glass. "Would you be a dear and fix me another?"

"Sure," I say.

I jump up, take her glass, and head toward the bar.

"The thing is . . ." Lexi says. "We have to thread a certain needle. We have a certain point of view, but we have to appear as if we don't, as if we're taking into account every side and then later conclude it was an accident and you and your friends are victims of that accident."

"Of course," Jamie says. "Fair and balanced."

"I bet your a Fox News watcher," Lexi says.

Jamie shrugs. "If I want anything it's that."

"You know how the talk shows have two guests so it appears both sides are considered?"

"Yeah."

"We have to do something like that."

"Sure, I get it."

Returning with her drink, I say, "The ME and the police have ruled the death an accident. That's not going to change. That's the truth. That's what we're reporting. That's the foundation of our show, but when we interview you on camera we need to hear you talk about any other factors that point to how and why family and friends and certain true crime fans believe it was murder."

She nods as she sips her drink.

As I sit back down, Lexi says, "And if you could reveal anything private or embarrassing, something most people wouldn't want to admit to it will make the audience trust you even more and give far more credibility to what you say."

"I could admit to having had work done," she says. "You know, joke about it."

"Sure," I say, "that would be good, but the more it has to do with Tracy and the party and what went on that night, the better."

"Oh, yeah, I see. I could talk about who had a beef and how much drugs and alcohol were bein' consumed."

"That's the goldmine right there," I say. "That's it."

Lexi says, "For instance . . . did Tracy really have a lot more to drink than everyone else?"

"No, of course not. She had a lot, but . . . we all did."

"Same true of drugs?"

"Sure. I mean, not everyone was doing either or both, but of the ones who were . . . they were doing a lot of what Tracy was doing. I just keep thinking what it would've been like if they had done toxicology tests on all of us."

"She had been smoking weed and had Xanax in her system and the police report makes it sound like she was the only one who was doing those things."

"Well, she wasn't. Not everyone was doing everything and maybe no one was doing anything as much as Tracy, but we were all doing plenty."

"That's the kind of revelations we need. The audience is going to love you for it," Lexi says.

I say, "Who did the weed belong to? What about the other drugs?"

"Couple of girls had the weed—Brandy and Tara, I believe. The Xanax was mine and Adeline has Adderall."

"That's good," Lexi says. "Just the sort of stuff we need to make a compelling show. What else you got for us?"

She finishes the last of her drink and without her asking I jump up, grab her glass, and quickly make her another.

"I could get use to this," she says.

Lexi says, "The more drama the better for the show. More people will tune in and your story will get out to more open-minded listeners."

"Let's see . . ." she says. "Always plenty of drama. Well . . ."

I hand her her drink and she takes a big gulp. "God, that's good."

Translation, it's strong as fuck and she's getting drunk.

"There was always drama with Steve and Adeline. They were fighting that night. He wasn't supposed to be there. And not only was he in the house but he was up there with us—and he had his loser friend with him. Addie was always scared he was goin' to try to fuck her friends."

"Steve or Ryan?"

"Well, both, but I was talking about Steve. Obviously, she cared more about him doin' it. I saw them arguing a lot. She went up to bed way before he did. I'm not sure they slept in the same room that night."

"Did he have any interaction with Tracy?"

"He was flirty as fuck with her, but I never saw them—I did see . . ."

"What?" Lexi says. "You did see what?"

"At some point Ryan made some comment that made Tracy and a few of the other girls upset."

"What kind of comment?" I ask.

"I can't remember. He made several. He was always talkin' shit. I'm sure he said something about blacks or women or something. Thing is . . . Tracy couldn't stand him. I mean, you could see the hostility comin' off her, but later that night in the back hallway by the bathroom I saw them . . . well, I don't know if they were kissing or if he kissed her before she knew what was happening. I only saw them for a moment in passing. I would've said they were making out, but I can't see her doing that with how much she hated him. He probably just surprised her, but when I saw them she didn't seem to be fighting him off. Least not that I could tell."

She's not slurring her words yet but there's a thickness to her speech as if her tongue has received the same injection as her lips.

"Later it got the more tension there was between Steve and Ryan. It was like they were both competing for Tracy or something. Not sure if it was because she was black or all energetic and high as hell or if it was because she was new. They always go after some strangers if there's any around."

"How did Adeline and the other women feel about that?" Lexi asks.

"They weren't happy. 'Specially Adeline. She called her husband to come get her but she wouldn't go. Keep thinkin' . . . if she had just gone with him she'd still be alive."

I start to say something but after a quick sip she continues.

"I'll tell you who was the most upset about all the attention Tracy was gettin' that night and that's Candi."

"That's Candi Tucker?" Lexi says.

"Yeah. No one knew it at the time, but she and Ryan had been hittin' it. So she was *jealous AF*. Wasn't too long after all this they got married."

"Ryan and Candi are married?" I say.

"I assume they still are. But you never know. Okay, I've got to go lay down. We'll talk more soon, but I'm all talked out for now and I need a nap."

She stands too quickly and drops her glass and is about to fall face-first on the deck, but I lunge toward her and catch her.

"Spilled my drinkypoo," she says. "Just help me to the couch. I don't feel like climbing the stairs."

We help her inside, ease her onto the couch, cover her with a blanket, and see ourselves out.

CHAPTER FOURTEEN

"YOU WERE VERY GOOD AT THAT," I say. "Thank you."

We are driving back into town from the beach, just coming off of Hathaway Bridge we are passing between Gulf Coast State College and the Panama City Port.

"It was fun," Lexi says.

She is driving and is doing so like she does most things—intensely. Weaving in and out of the slower traffic, she seems to have transferred the focus she had been using on interviewing Jamie onto her driving.

Observing the way she ran circles around Jamie and watching her driving circles around all the other vehicles on the road I'm even more attracted to her than usual.

"It was easy," I say. "Wish all interviewees were that talkative."

"Yeah. Sure was a lot goin' on that night."

"And none of the tea she spilled today is in the police reports or witness statements."

"Of course not. Conspiracy of silence. If a man who wasn't even supposed to be there assaulted or raped her and then killed her to cover it up . . . Or if his jealous girlfriend shoved her off the balcony . . . And that same scenario could be true not just of Ryan and Candi but Steve and Adeline."

"Yes it could."

"And there's other motives too," she says. "Lots of them. And if they were mixing all their drugs with oceans of alcohol . . . No tellin' what really happened."

"Hope we'll be able to tell eventually," I say.

"You will."

I want her so badly. With our twenty-four-hour protection on Alana and Ashlynn we haven't had much time to be intimate lately. Nor a place to have it in.

"Do you have time for a quickie somewhere?" I ask. "My place is out. People are there watching Ashlynn and Alana, but we could grab a room at a no-tell motel or something."

"Oh, I'd love that," she says.

"Want to make a return engagement to the Bay Breeze?"

We had used the Bay Breeze for fun when working a case not too long ago that took us there.

"Sounds so seedily amazing."

"Let's do it."

I'm equal parts turned on and thrilled to be able to do something about it.

"Hey," she says, "I've got something I need to tell you."

"Sounds ominous."

"It's not. Sorry to make it sound that way. It's just . . . now that we're more casual than we were—or than I thought we were—and you're seeing other people . . . I just wanted you to know that I am too. God help me I've signed up for a few dating apps and I'm getting some interest."

"Of course you are," I say. "You're a fuckin' catch."

Suddenly, I feel deflated, my amorousness and excitement drained. And it's not even that I'm upset about her dating other guys or that I don't think she should. I'm not sure why I'm feeling what I'm feeling. Probably just my initial, visceral reaction to the news. I'm sure I'll adjust to it soon enough but in this moment I feel sad and alone and incapable of intimacy.

"Didn't want to make a big deal of it because it's not, but I also didn't want to not tell you because . . ."

"Because," I say, "browsing can always turn to buying."

"I guess. I don't see that happening but you never know. I just wanted to tell you while it was early days. Didn't want . . . I just wanted you to know."

"I appreciate that."

"We good?"

I nod. "We are. Thank you for telling me. I appreciate you being so . . . I appreciate you . . . your character."

"I want to move forward with you when you're ready or when we feel like we can," she says. "And I don't want to fuck things up before then."

I nod, then fake getting a text.

"Ah, damn," I say, "I've got to get back to the office. I've got to relieve Bobby Doll and watch Alana this afternoon."

"Really?"

"Yeah. Sorry."

"Not even time for a super quick quickie?"

"Sorry. I'll check with you later this afternoon or tonight to see if we can slip away then if you're available."

"This isn't because of what I said, is it?"

"No," I lie. "Of course not.

"You sure? The timing seems . . ."

"I know, but it's not. I'm glad you're getting out there. I am."

"Okay," she says. "Damn, I'm disappointed."

"Me too."

CHAPTER FIFTEEN

"HOW HAVE YOU BEEN?" I ask.

She shrugs. "Okay, I guess."

That evening I meet Destiny Diamonds at the Salty Hobo.

Billing itself as Panama City's premiere dive bar, the Salty Hobo is a dim, funkily decorated bar in what used to be the Watershed with a magnificent view of St. Andrew Bay.

"Sorry I haven't called you sooner," I say. "I've been out of town on business."

When Logan Owens had me to investigate her the first time, I had gone to see her at Cloud Nine Gentlemen's Club. After tipping her on the stage, she came over to see me at my table and we had eventually wound up in a VIP room in the back where she gave me the girlfriend experience and her number. I had no intention of ever using her number but was glad I had it when I was put back on her case. Not only does Dimitri own Cloud Nine but his office is in the back so he's there most of the time.

I'm not even sure what Destiny's real name is. The name she gave on her voicemail was Heather but the way she said it sounded fake.

Destiny or Heather or whoever is meeting me on her way to work. She's a tall, thin, leggy platinum blonde with plenty of long hair extensions, massive fake mammaries, a smooth airbrush spray tan, and makeup that appears professionally applied.

"Yeah, I was bummed when you didn't call," she says. "I really thought we had a connection."

"We did," I lie. "It was so intense it scared me a little bit."

"I get that," she says. "But . . . the only thing to be scared of is missin' out, you know? Not following the lead of love."

We are at a long table in the backroom where a DJ is spinning 80s tunes. There's a pop-up art market on the front porch and there are people out there as well as in the main room at the bar, but we're the only patrons in here.

The room we're in is painted black, including the ceiling, and has white graffiti artwork and quotes all over. A pair of partial mannequins are inside the fireplace on the south wall.

The DJ, Crescent Cat out of New Orleans, fades "You Spin Me Round" into "Time After Time."

"I just figured you . . . in your position . . . have that with a lot of guys."

"It's rare. It truly is. I love this song. Let's dance."

She springs up, grabs my hand, and pulls me onto the dance floor.

I press my body into hers and we fall into the rhythm of the song.

We slow dance but the beat of the song is faster than it first seems, so we move pretty quickly to the melancholic 80s synth pop.

Her movements are sensual and sexual and the way she kisses my neck and whispers in my ear it's like we're back in the VIP room at Cloud Nine.

When the song ends, Crescent Cat gives us a shoutout and bows toward us and we stumble back to our table.

I'm revved up and wishing I hadn't let the news that Lexi is starting to date keep me from going to a hotel with her this afternoon.

"Are you involved with anyone at the moment?" I ask.

She shrugs. "No one special."

I can tell she thinks I'm asking because of the experience she just gave me on the dance floor.

"I bet they think they're special," I say.

She shrugs. "Probably."

"I think I saw you two together a while back," I say. "If it's who I think it is he's a dangerous guy."

She shrugs again and says in her most resigned voice, "I learned a long time ago most are."

"It's not most," I say. "It's really not. But in your line of work it's best to assume all are."

"Including you?" she asks, her manner playful and flirtatious.

I nod. "Including me."

"You're not dangerous," she says. "I know dangerous and it ain't you."

"What would you do if he asked you to marry him?"

"Who?"

"Your boyfriend."

"I don't have boyfriend."

"Your boyfriend thinks you do."

"Huh?"

"I"m just saying I bet he thinks you do. And I wouldn't be surprised if he proposed."

"I get proposals all the time."

"I'm sure you do," I say. "I just worry about the way some guys handle rejection."

"Yeah, I know what you mean. The male ego. I try to let 'em down gently."

"Good."

"But if you're too worried about it . . . you could always propose and take me off the market."

It's hard to tell how serious she is. I hope she's not but I'm afraid she is."

"But that's what I mean . . . Say I propose and you accept—"

"Won't know until you ask."

"—What would the guy who thinks you're his girlfriend and was about to ask you to marry him do? Probably be acid to the face for you and a bullet to the head for me."

"Where is all this coming from?" she asks. "You seem to have thought about this a lot."

"I just worry about you," I say.

"That's sweet, but I'll be okay. And now I've got to go and all we did was talk about yucky ol' mean men."

"Next time we won't," I say.

"Okay, I'm gonna hold you to both of those."

"Both?"

"That there'll be a next time and you won't talk about losers the whole time."

CHAPTER SIXTEEN

COURTNEY KNOX IS a realtor in Panama City Beach, and though she's about eight years older than us, we met her in the system as kids.

She is a short, plumpish black woman with lots and lots of curly hair.

Perpetually in a dress and high heels, when she moves she waddles more than walks.

"This is the house where the black woman at the all-white slumber party died," she says.

I nod.

"Who y'all workin' for?"

"The husband and stepdaughter."

"Hope y'all can get her some kind of justice."

"Some kind is all there is," Blade says. "And we will."

"I've got to be here with you in case the owners or another realtor shows up. Want to start with the inside or outside?"

I look over at Blade.

"We already outside," she says.

The four-story beach house is just west of Pier Park and only a few houses down from Jamie Hodgins'.

We're standing on the cement parking area, a portion of

which is covered by an attached carport. The front door, which is on this level, is actually the second floor. Wooden steps lead up to it and a wooden deck that wraps around both sides leads to the large wooden deck in the back.

The exterior of the house, which is painted in beachy pastels of moss green with highlights of pale yellow, is enormous and the crows nest office on the fourth floor is crowned by a gold cupola.

"Owners are goin' through a divorce," Courtney says. "Neither of them live here, but there's a security system, so if they still monitor it they'll know every time we open and close a door and if the cameras work they'll be able to see everything we do, so . . . we need to be quick and look like we're looking at the property as potential buyers not private investigators."

"Hopefully, they're not actually monitoring it," I say, "but you're right . . . we need to be quick and careful."

"Damn cameras weren't workin' the night Tracy was killed," Blade says. "But I'm sure they workin' now."

"Let's start with the back deck where they say she fell from," I say.

We climb the three stairs that lead up to the front door, but instead of entering the house we turn right and follow the narrow wooden walkway of the wrap-around porch to the large observation deck in the back.

The huge deck is as wide as the house and extends nearly twenty feet into the sand dunes. Unlike Jamie's deck, this one is empty.

"There's usually a few tables and chairs and a few chaise lounges out here," Courtney says.

"Yeah," I say, "that's what was out here that night. The table closest to the railing had a pack of cigarettes, a lighter, and bottle of booze all with only Tracy's prints on them."

We walk over to the railing and look down.

We focus on the spot in the sand about ten feet directly in front of us where Tracy's body was found.

Blade starts shaking her head immediately. "No way a fall from this height killed her. Even if she was standing on the rail."

The distance down to the ground in less than fifteen feet and the surface below is sand.

"Not only is it hard to see a twelve foot fall onto sand killing her," I say, "but this railing is too high and substantial for her to accidentally stumble over."

The wooden railing is sturdy and solid, and includes multiple boards as well as thick flat one across the top, which is wide enough to stand on if someone were daring enough to climb up to it. The height of the railing is somewhere between four and four and a half feet. I'm six feet—several inches taller than Tracy—and there's no way I could accidentally fall over the railing.

Blade says, "Do you think even if you were standing on the railing that you could jump far enough to land where she did?"

I shake my head. "Don't think so."

"Let's take a look at the downstairs and ground," Blade says.

We cross the deck to the black metal stairs on the east side of the balcony and descend them.

The stairs lead down to a covered patio beneath the upper deck. Large glass sliding doors lead into the dark game room.

We walk over to the patio and look out.

"Don't forget to look like we're looking at the view," Courtney says.

Bordering the patio is a one-foot bed of decorative rocks covering a drainage system below. Beyond which is only sand and sea.

I point to it. "Initially, because of the visible scrapes and scratches to her shins, the first cops on the scene thought she was down here and just tripped or passed out and fell over into the sand, scraping her legs on these rocks as she did."

"Which is ridiculous," Courtney says. "Totally absurd."

I nod. "The impact from stumbling to the ground is not enough to kill you—and certainly doesn't explain all her internal injuries. Plus, her body wasn't found here. It was found about ten feet out that way in the sand—which, even that seems too far from a fall off the balcony."

"None of this shit adds up," Blade says.

"How the hell they get away with ruling it an accident is what I want to know," Courtney says.

"You know how," Blade says.

"And because they treated like an accident," I say, "there was very little investigation. Very few crime scene photos. Very few notes. And the witness statements are a joke."

"Y'all ready to look inside?" Courtney asks.

CHAPTER SEVENTEEN

WE WALK BACK up the stairs, around to the front, and enter the house through the large, solid wood door with the iron knocker on it.

We pass quickly through the tile floor entryway and into the great room.

The enormous room has two different seating areas with couches, loveseats, and chairs, a dining area, a full bar, a large kitchen with an island and a bar with large, heavily padded barstools in front of it.

Everything is pristine, immaculate, and expensive.

Blade shakes her head. "This ain't even they only house."

"They have a lot to protect," Courtney says, "and the resources to protect it. No way they gonna let the death of some black condo cleaner mess this up."

"So," I say, "they're hanging out in here. Drinking. Talking. Eating. And at some point the two guys come up. And instead of grabbing food and going back down to the game room they stay and join in."

"Even though nobody wanted them to," Blade says. "Including Adeline."

In front of us are the two sliding glass doors beyond which is the balcony the police concluded Tracy fell from.

"So . . . according to the witness statements not only was Tracy drinking more than anyone she was the only one going out onto the balcony to smoke—and not just cigarettes. In and out all night long. But we now know she often had someone with her. And every time anyone went out those doors—or any doors—in the house the security system logged it."

"I doubt she ever went out there or anywhere else alone," Blade says. "Including the last time."

To our right is a hallway leading down to a bathroom and a couple of guest rooms.

"Jamie says that both men were flirting with Tracy and that she actually saw Ryan kissing her at the end of this hallway by the bathroom. And since they so quickly assumed it was an accident they didn't order a rape kit."

"'Course they didn't. 'Sides . . . it's not rape if it's a nigger."

Her words are like a slap across the face and we're all silent a moment.

Eventually, Courtney says, "Y'all gonna get justice for her."

Blade shakes her head. "No such thing. Not for the victim."

Courtney frowns and nods.

"But," Blade says, "we *are* gonna find the fucker or fuckers who did this and rain down a little justice on they asses, okay?"

"Well, okay, then."

Blade looks at me. "I've been thinking. This bitch is four stories, right? What if she was pushed or thrown from higher up?"

"Her injuries would make more sense."

"Come this way," Courtney says.

She leads us back into the foyer and to the staircase on the left side.

On what is the second floor in the front and third floor in the back, we find three bedrooms, two bathrooms, and a reading nook with built-in bookcases next to the stairs. Only one of the rooms has a balcony. Courtney opens the French doors and we step out onto it. It's relatively small, maybe ten feet long and about five feet wide.

When we reach the railing, we lean over and look down.

"Well, hell," Blade says. "There goes that theory."

The deck below is so large if someone fell or was even pushed or thrown, they would land on the deck, not ten feet beyond it in the sand.

"It was a good thought."

"Same is probably gonna be true of the crow's nest but let's take a look at it," Courtney says.

She leads us up a narrower flight of stairs into a smallish office.

Opening the single exterior door, she steps aside so we can walk out onto the balcony.

The deck up here is even smaller and there's no way a falling body would land anywhere but on the deck below.

"Blade says, "Even with two men swinging her and flinging her as far as they could . . . she'd still land on the deck below. *Fuck.*"

We step back inside and Courtney closes and locks the door.

We make our way back down the narrow staircase, through the third floor, and down to the second-story landing next to the reading area.

"Why couldn't she have been thrown from up there and landed on the balcony?" Courtney asks. "And then they moved her."

"No way to hide an impact like that," I say. "The boards would show where she fell and she'd have different injuries and splinters in her skin. One of the few investigative things they actually did was have the FDLE crime scene techs check the balcony for blood. There wasn't any."

"Then maybe it really was an accident and she fell from the balcony somehow," she says. "Maybe with all the booze and drugs in her system . . ."

Blade shakes her head. "Doesn't add up."

"Sometimes shit doesn't," Courtney says.

Downstairs the front door opens and someone walks into the foyer.

Courtney's eyes grow wide and she quickly turns and heads back down the stairs.

We follow.

CHAPTER EIGHTEEN

"JIG'S UP," Ryan Bowman says. "Steve recognized you. Y'all ain't interested in buying this place. You're tryin' to get even more notoriety by usin' this tragic accident for your own selfish gain. Now get the fuck out of here before I call the cops."

Courtney, who is visibly nervous, says, "Sir, I assure you I'm a legitimate real estate agent and—"

"Nobody said you weren't," he says, "but if you want to remain one you better get these two political whores the hell out of here."

"It's interesting Steve called you instead of the cops," I say.

Bowman is a bodybuilder. His head, which is probably average sized looks small compared to the rest of his roid-raging, overdeveloped body. His coarse dark hair is closely cropped to his average-sized head and beneath it the dark skin of his forehead is deeply furrowed. He looks Hispanic but his accent is strictly Deep South North Florida.

Blade says, "Tell you what I've learned doin' this work. Innocent people don't mind you investigating, but guilty bitches always try and stop you."

"Investigate all you like," he says. "Just get the hell out of here. And we *are* innocent. Everyone of us. But we're treated like criminals. We're called every name in the book. We're harassed. We've lost our jobs. To this day we still get death threats. *Death threats.* Because that black bitch didn't know how to pace herself and did a header off the balcony."

"Interesting you should say that," I say. "Because if she had done a header as you say she would've broken her neck and her body would've been in a different position. That would've been believable. But that's not what happened."

"We don't claim to know what happened or be able to explain it," he says. "We just had nothing to do with it. Put yourself in our place. We wake up to find her dead. Can we tell you exactly what happened? No. We were asleep. We had nothing to do with it. And because we had nothing to do with it and don't know anything about it . . . we're accused of lying and covering up and being guilty of something we had nothing to do with."

"If that's the case," I say, "that's what our report will say."

"We got no dog in this fight," Blade says. "We not tryin' to prove anything. We just searching for the truth."

"But," I add, "that's not something we can ever get at if y'all keep blocking us from investigating."

"Again," he says, "not blockin' you from investigating. Just tellin' you to get off private property. Y'all tryin' to come off all righteous but y'all are here under false pretenses."

"Are there any other kind?" I say.

"Huh?"

"Nothin."

As we've been talking, Courtney has slowly backed away so she's now several feet behind us.

Ryan says, "If y'all really wanted to get at the truth you'd come at us straight. Ask for an interview. Request to a tour of the house. Not sneak in here like your broke asses lookin' to buy the place."

"That sounds good in theory," I say, "but we've discovered lie after lie in the witness statements and interviews y'all gave."

Blade says, "Truth is a two-way street. You want us to come at y'all straight but y'all ain't bein' straight with anybody."

"I don't know exactly what everybody said . . . but I'd be shocked if anybody did anything but downplay how much drinkin' and druggin' they did."

"And we'd understand if it's just that," I say, "but we can't know it's just that without investigating."

"And if you claimin' to be a truth teller," Blade says. "Tell us the truth about this . . . We have a witness who says you assaulted Tracy."

"Bullshit," he says. "That's total BS. See? That's the kind of shit I'm talkin' about. You can't say shit like that and—"

"We're not saying it," I say. "We're tellin' you that one of your fellow party goers said it and we're asking for your side."

"I've never assaulted anyone," he says. "I've never . . . hurt anyone. Not ever. That's not who I am."

Blade says, "You're here threatening us."

"No, I said I'd call the cops. People see all these muscles and they think I'm a . . . I don't know . . . enforcer type. But I'm not. I work out. But I don't bully people. I . . . I'll tell you what I did. I . . . I was drinkin' like everybody else and I . . . I misread some signals. She was being all flirty and shit and I thought . . . All I did was kiss her. She said she wasn't available, that she loved her husband and I apologized and that was that."

"How do you know?" Blade says.

"How do I know what?"

"If you were so drunk you misread signals and kissed someone who didn't want you to, how do you know it stopped there?"

"I wasn't wasted," he says. "I was just a little loose. I know what I did and did not do. Check the security footage. Ask anyone who has ever had any interaction with me. Ask them if I've ever forced myself on anyone."

"We were told there wasn't any security footage," I say.

"There wasn't of her fall," he says. "The exterior cameras

were offline, but the interior ones worked just fine. I didn't assault anyone. Look at the footage."

"We'd like to," I say. "Can you get it for us?"

He squints and looks away as he seems to think about it. "I'm tellin' the truth. And the footage proves it. Also proves nobody killed her, but . . . you or anyone else could cut that footage together to make it look like anything—including that I killed her."

That's not exactly true, but I know what he means. It could be edited to make someone appear more suspicious. That happens all the time on true crime shows when they take a particular point of view.

"How 'bout this?" I say. "You show it to us. Not just the part that proves you didn't assault Tracy, but all of the footage. You don't give it to us. You just let us watch it. Uncut. Every frame."

He seems to think about that. Eventually, he begins to nod slowly. "I could probably do that. You couldn't have your phones or anything."

"No problem. Do you have all the footage?

He nods. "Yeah. As soon as all the accusations began to fly Steve and I both got a copy and gave a copy to the cop in charge."

"It's not mentioned in the file."

"I bet there's a lot of shit not mentioned in the file," he says. "He had his own way of doin' things, but . . . whatever is or isn't in the file . . . it all comes to the same thing. That poor woman died in a tragic accident and wasn't killed by any of us."

CHAPTER NINETEEN

"YOU BELIEVE HIM?" Blade asks.

"Be far more likely to if he shows us the uncut security footage."

We are back in the car but still in the driveway. Courtney has just pulled out onto 98.

"It's too convenient that the exterior cameras weren't working that night."

I nod. "Damn sure is."

"And we supposed to believe a roid head like him just a big ol' teddy bear?"

"Side effects may include misreading signals and unwanted kissing."

She laughs.

"You know," I say, "we're just a few doors down from Jamie's place and it's after the cocktail hour."

"*Shee-it,* twenty-four cocktail hour at her place."

"I'm thinkin' we dip in and see how loose her lips are now."

She smiles. "They loose all the time. Trust me. I know what I'm talkin' about."

I turn around in the wide driveway and pull up to the street. When traffic clears, I ease onto 98.

"It's possible it was an accident," I say. "I don't think it's likely, but . . . I'm not ready to rule it out yet."

"We won't rule it out until we prove it was something else."

I nod.

She says, "Be hard to prove it was an accident."

"Be more about disproving everything else."

"Yeah, guess so. But . . . don't see that happenin'. Case leads we follow and shit, but . . . I'll be surprised as hell if one of them didn't off her."

"One or more," I say.

I pull into Jamie Hodgins' driveway and park.

We get out and instead of ringing the front doorbell, we walk around the side of the house to the back.

We find Jamie passed out on one of the couches, her head dangerously close to the fire pit.

I ease her up and she opens her eyes. "It's . . . the TV people. I'm . . . ready . . . close-up."

"You okay?" I ask.

"Just takin' . . . little nappy poo."

Blade says, "Almost caught your hairy poo on fire."

"Hey," Jamie says. "Hey. Hey. I . . . thought of . . . something . . . What was it? Wait. It'll . . . come to me."

"Was it about—"

"Oh, yeah," she says. "Beds."

The waves of the unseen Gulf and the wind whipping around make it even more difficult to understand her.

"Beds?"

"Yeah."

"What about them?" I ask.

"Upstairs."

"Beds upstairs," I say. "What—"

"Not . . . enough. Could . . . I have . . . water?"

Blade quickly moves over to the bar, grabs a bottle of water, and brings it to her.

She has trouble removing the cap. I reach down and help her.

"Thanks."

She lifts the bottle and guzzles a third of it down.

"So . . . parched. That's better."

Her voice is clearer now.

"Not enough," she says.

"Beds upstairs?" I ask.

"Yeah."

"Okay."

"Tara," she says.

"Barnes?" I ask.

She nods and drinks more water.

"Tara," she says. "She . . . slept . . . downstairs."

"Where?" I ask.

"Game room," she says.

"Tara Barnes slept down in the game room?"

She nods. "Yes. Yes. Yes."

"Okay."

"She . . . heard . . . thought she . . . heard . . . an argument up on the balcony . . . middle of the night."

I glance at Blade who gives me a wide-eyed expression.

"That's good," I say. "It's not in any of the reports or statements."

"She told . . . Mike."

"Mike Reeves, the investigator," I say.

"Yeah. Yes."

"She was havin' an affair with him at the time, wasn't she?"

"Yes," she says, nodding vigorously. "Yes . . . she was."

"So," Blade says, "she hears an argument on the balcony in the middle of the night and tells the lead investigator, who she's schtuppin', and he buries it?"

"Can you help us talk to Tara?" I ask.

"Yeah, sure. Where's . . . my phone."

"Not now, but soon," I say. "When you're feeling better. We'll set up a meeting."

Blade says, "Now, let's get you inside so you don't burn your hair off."

CHAPTER TWENTY

ALANA and I are at my kitchen table having an art contest she will inevitably win.

The table, very little of which can be seen, holds piles of paper—of both the copy and construction variety—a couple of pairs of scissors, three different types of tape, jars of silver and gold glitter, and a rainbow of random pencils, pens, markers, and crayons.

She talks to herself and me as she works.

"Don't look at what I'm making," she says.

"I'm not."

"And don't copy."

"Can't copy if I don't look and I'm not looking."

"Can we let Mommy and Blade judge these when they get back?"

Blade and Ashlynn are out grabbing a few household supplies and ingredients to make dinner.

"Sure."

"Can we hang the winner on the fridge?" she asks.

"Of course."

My phone vibrates on the table beside me. It's Pete saying he's about to come in and not to shoot.

A few moments later, he unlocks the door and walks in.

"Not another art contest," he says as he joins us at the table.

"Yep," Alana says.

"I'm not sure how many more losses Burke's self-esteem can take."

"Maybe he'll win this time," she says.

When her full attention returns to her work, Pete looks at me and lowers his voice.

"I gave that Losif character to organized crime," he says. "Says he's willing to wear a wire. Doubt it'll come to anything but you never know."

"He'll never get close enough to get anything," I say. "And if he does get close enough to even have a conversation . . . he'll never get Dimitri to cop to anything."

"Yeah, that's what I figure. But it's worth a shot."

"Which is probably what Losif's gonna get."

He laughs. "True."

"Color something, Pete," Alana says.

"Yes, ma'am."

He grabs a random crayon closest to him and half-heartedly begins to draw stick figures on a partial sheet of printer paper.

"How's the other thing coming?" he asks.

I shrug. "We're gettin' there."

"I got the printout of the security alerts."

"Thanks. "Did you know there's footage from the inside cameras from that night?"

He shakes his head. "I didn't think there was any camera footage at all. Just the doors opens and closes logs. Nothing like that was logged into evidence."

"Ryan Bowman is supposed to be getting it for us."

"Really? Why?"

"To prove he didn't assault the victim."

"If he didn't be good to know."

I nod.

"You still seeing Lexi?" he asks.

I shrug. "Some."

Alana continues to focus on her colorful creation, seeming oblivious to us, but I know she's taking in every word.

"Just haven't seen her around as much lately."

I cut my eyes over at Alana. "We've got a lot goin' on right now, so . . . not as much time for other things. Besides . . . until I'm off probation . . . it's not like she's really available."

"Thought that was the whole point."

"What was?" I ask.

"Unavailability."

I smile. "You in another support group?"

In the past few years, Pete has turned to self-help and self-care practices, counseling, and support groups and like all new converts to every religion feels the burden to evangelize and proselytize any chance he gets.

"We all need to be," he says. "We're . . . think about the trauma we've all been through. We were all abandoned . . . and now our fear of abandonment informs everything we do."

He's not wrong and he means well and I try not to get too defensive.

"How's it workin' for you?" I ask. "You lost all your fear of abandonment and find yourself with secure attachments in healthy, non-codependent relationships?"

He gives me a little nod and a you-got-me smirk. "Not yet, no."

"I know what you're sayin's right," I say. "My anger management programs are Twelve Steps-based. And they work—if you work them. And maybe one day I can get to my attachment and abandonment issues. Right now I'm tryin' to deal with my rage so I can be out here to help keep our family safe instead of in prison."

"I know. I don't mean to be . . . I know you're workin' on shit—"

Alana says, "Ooooh, Uncle Pete used a bad word."

"Sorry," he says. "Stuff. I know you're workin' on stuff and I . . . it's just all related."

"Yes it is."

"I didn't mean to—"

"I appreciate your concern. I do. Don't stop sharing."

He nods. "Thanks. And if you ever want to go to a meeting with me . . ."

"Thanks."

Alana says, "Can y'all stop with all the talky talky and start drawing?"

We can and we do.

And a little while later Blade and Ashlynn return and we cook and eat dinner together, our little makeshift family with insecure attachment styles and fear of abandonment.

CHAPTER TWENTY-ONE

TARA BARNES IS the branch manager of the Gulf Coast Community Credit Union in Callaway, which is located on the east side of Panama City not far from Tyndall Air Force Base.

Driving over to see her we witnessed again all the ways this area still hasn't recovered from Hurricane Michael, the Cat 5 superstorm that pummeled the region back in October of 2018. Boarded-up businesses, blue roofs, their frayed tarps flapping in the wind, and vacant lots where once were stores or homes creating a sad, snaggled-tooth landscape.

The small credit union lobby is mostly empty—one customer stands at the teller counter depositing the contents of a blue bank bag.

We find Tara in her office, which is professional but plain and impersonal.

She's a late-forties brunette whose hair and large glasses are a few years out of style. She's wearing a gray, single-breasted skirt suit with a white blouse, the well-worn clothes struggling to hold her large breasts and extra pounds in check.

She flashes us a fake smile and says, "Good morning. How can I help you two today?"

I say, "We're interested in transferring our business accounts over here."

"I can certainly help you with that," she says.

"Can you tell us what you offer?"

"Sure," she says, and launches into the benefits of banking with her. Several minutes into her spiel she asks, "What sort of business do you have?"

"A private detective agency," I say.

She nods slowly and says, "I thought you looked familiar. Y'all found that missing girl. Y'all are famous."

"We're actually working a case right now that you might be able to help us with," I say.

Panic fills her face and she sits back a bit and becomes guarded.

"Blade says, "We're taking a second look at what happened to Tracy Adams. We understand you heard an argument from up on the balcony around the time she died."

"What? No. I never said that. Who told you that?"

"Why don't you tell us what you really said," I say.

She shakes her head. "This is never going away, is it? It's going to follow us for the rest of our lives and—"

"It won't if we can solve it once and for all," I say. "We will share our conclusions—whether it's accident, suicide, or homicide—when we finish our investigation and that will be the end of it."

"Y'all don't really want to open an account, do you?"

I say, "You tell us the truth about what really happened that night and we will move all our business and personal banking here."

She shakes her head. "I don't know . . . I hate talkin' about it. And I've been told not to."

"By who?" Blade asks.

She shakes her head. "Doesn't matter."

"Look," I say. "We already know you heard something.

Rather than us getting it wrong in our report just tell us what really happened. No harm in that. Set the record straight."

"Will you . . . Can you leave my name out of it?"

I nod. "Sure," I lie. "No problem."

"Who you scared of?" Blade asks.

"No one. Just don't need no publicity. My job is . . . My boss is very conservative and believes bankers must be above reproach to earn the trust of the community."

I can tell she's using his words not hers.

"We understand," I say. "This is just background for our investigation. We'll leave you out of it."

She seems to consider that and then nods slowly.

"I wish I'd've never gone to that damn party," she says. "I'm a little older than the rest of them. Didn't have a kid playing ball. I was . . . Well, I was trying to get Steve and Adeline's business."

I nod. "I'm sure that's a big part of your job, bringing in new clients."

"All the bedrooms upstairs were occupied," she says. "I could've shared a bed, but I didn't want to. And that Ryan guy gave me the creeps, so . . . I decided to crash in the game room. I grabbed a blanket and pillow from upstairs and went down to the game room, locked the door, and sacked out on one of the couches."

Blade and I both nod and encourage her to continue.

"I didn't drink nearly as much as the others, but I was definitely buzzed and I slept hard but fitful and kept waking up. At some point, I heard an argument from upstairs. I have—"

"What time was that?" I ask.

She frowns and shakes her head. "I didn't look at my phone, so I have no idea. But I didn't get down there until close to two."

"Who was it?" I ask.

"No idea. And I can't tell you whether it was in the house or on the balcony."

"Was it a man and a woman or two women or what?"

"The voices were muffled. Not sure."

"Could you make out any words?"

"No," she says, shaking her head again. "They were yelling I know that, but that's about all. Sounded angry and . . . I don't know."

"Did you hear anything else?" I ask.

"A couple of thuds, maybe. I really can't be sure now what is memory and what is . . . I just don't know anymore."

"But it sounded like a fight?"

She shrugs. "Maybe, but I'd say more like an argument. That's all I know."

"You tell anybody?" Blade asks. "Anybody official?"

She nods. "Yeah."

"Mike Reed?" I ask "The investigator in charge?"

She nods.

"You two were close, weren't you?"

She was one of the women Reed was having an affair with.

She shakes her head. "Not at the time."

"But you got close after that," I say. "Started seeing each other."

"I don't want to talk about that," she says. "I won't."

"Does he scare you?" I ask.

"I've told y'all all I know," she says. "I need to get back to work. Please, please leave my name out of it."

"We will," I say. "And here's my card. If anyone harasses or threatens you or you feel scared give us a call."

"I feel scared all the time," she says. "I can't call you all the time."

CHAPTER TWENTY-TWO

WHEN WE GET BACK to our office, Nate and Luna are waiting for us.

Like the last time we saw them, they look like they're from two different worlds—his blue-collar, hers glamorous, his practical, hers fanciful.

Today she's in a pair of pale blue high-rise, wide-bottomed pants and a pale pink wife beater, both of which are distressed and paint spattered. She has no bra on beneath the wife beater and her large breasts have large, protruding nipples that are driving me to distraction.

Nate is in a pair of dusty, grass-covered jeans, weathered work boots, a navy-blue hoodie, and a matching navy-blue ball cap.

"We wanted to check on your progress," she says in her soft voice. "See how things were going and if you needed anything else from us."

"Come on in," I say.

The four of us walk through the lobby to our office.

After we're all seated—Blade on the corner of the desk, me in the chair behind it, and the two of them in the client chairs across from it—I say, "We're making progress for sure, but it's early days. We haven't even interviewed everyone yet."

"We gettin' more cooperation than we thought we would," Blade says.

"Really?" Luna says, her voice rising in pitch. "That's really surprising. Wasn't expecting that."

"Some of it comin' from those who want to help," she says. "Some of it comin' 'cause we tricked 'em or . . ." She glances at me.

"Cajoled," I say.

"'Cause we cajoled they asses," she says. "But cooperation is cooperation."

"That's great."

Nate clears his throat and says, "From what you've learned so far . . . are you leanin' more toward accident or . . . her bein' killed?"

"Like I said we've just getting started good, but . . . the more we learn the less likely we think it could've been an accident."

He nods. "That's . . . good."

"That's him bein' all careful and shit," Blade says. "'Cause it could still turn out to be an accident or we might not be able to prove what it is, but I'll tell y'all that I'm about as certain as I can be at this point that she was murdered."

"The thing is . . ." Nate says. "I . . . I don't know how to say this, but we're broke. We don't have any more money to pay you. Tracy didn't have any life insurance or anything. Took every penny we had just to bury her."

Luna says, "The money I paid you with was the last of my left over scholarship money for this semester. I . . . I guess I was hoping . . . Well, I know what I was hoping—either you'd be able to solve it real quick or that Dad would kick in when the retainer ran out or you'd get so committed to the case that you'd want to stay on to finish it even when we weren't able to pay you any longer."

I nod. "I appreciate your honesty."

"Nate," Blade says, "how many yards you cut because you got so committed to making the yard look good even though the homeowners said they couldn't pay you anymore?"

"None. And that's not what I'm asking y'all to do."

"This is all me," Luna says. "He didn't even know I hired y'all in the first place. I was desperate and I'm sorry."

Nate clears his throat, but the tension in his voice remains. "Why don't y'all just go as far as you can until the retainer runs out and then write us a report on what you find. And in the future if we have the money we'll hire you to pick up where you left off."

Blade nods. "We can do that."

"I shoulda known," Mike Reeves says as he enters our office. "'Course it's y'all that hired them."

He's a tall and thick white man in his late forties or early fifties, cowboy boots and a cowboy hat at either end of his beige sheriff's uniform.

"I came to tell you two to stay the fuck out of my case," he says to me and Blade. Then looking at Luna and Nate adds, "Shoulda known I'd find you two here."

"'Less you want to answer some questions about the case," Blade says, "you need to go. This is private property and you're trespassing."

"I'll go when I get good and goddamn ready to," he says. "And not a minute before."

Blade smiles. "That's where you're wrong. We'll toss your fat cracker ass out if we have to."

"You even try—'cause that's all you could do is try—and I'll arrest you for assault on a law enforcement officer."

"You may have a little power over in that little county you sheriff of but you got no jurisdiction here. This is private property and you're trespassing."

"Let me tell you something you uppity little . . . I'm not someone you want as an enemy. If you so much as look at anyone involved in my case . . . I'm gonna rain down misery on your life like you can't imagine. Stop harassing the victims of this case. They've all been through enough. Stop taking these poor grievin' people's money and go fuck up some other case that'll get your picture in the paper."

He turns his attention to Nate and Luna. "And you two. You need to get on with your lives. It was a terrible tragic accident. Wanting it to be something else will never change that. All you're doin' is wasting your money and your time. Let it go and move on."

"If you'd done your damn job none of us would have to be here doin' this now," Luna says.

"I'm gonna cut you some slack, young lady, 'cause I know you're upset about your mom, but be careful how you talk to me. I'm warnin' all of you . . . let this go. Move on. Stay away from my case. Stay away from the players involved. Now, I've said what I came to say, so I'm leaving—but only because I'm ready to."

CHAPTER TWENTY-THREE

TODAY NATASHA LEONE'S coffee truck, Mug Shots, is at the end of Beck Avenue in St. Andrews in the parking lot of the Tap Room.

I'm walking there to see her when Clyde pulls up next to me in a dark ash-gray metallic Chevy Tahoe with illegally tinted windows so black nothing can be seen inside.

Rolling down the window, he says, "Mr. Owens is in the back. He wants to talk to you. Get in."

It's a violation of my probation to be anywhere near Logan Owens but I open the back door and get in.

The huge vehicle is spacious and comfortable, its climate perfectly controlled.

I sink into the leather seat and glance over at Owens.

He is a young, thin, pale white man with freakishly light blue eyes and wild bleached-blond hair. He's wearing dark shades and staring straight ahead.

I have a strong urge to reach over and strangle him with my barehands. I resist it.

Obviously, the anger management counseling is working.

Apart from a brief random encounter at a bar called the Lie'Brary and a confrontation in my apartment where he set me up to get video footage he could blackmail me with, this is the only time I've been around him since my trial when his award-worthy performance helped send me to prison.

"Clyde has relayed your information about Destiny," he says, "but I want to hear it from you."

"She's not having an affair," I say.

It's surreal to be sitting here talking to the predator I hospitalized and who in turn sent me to prison and is now blackmailing me with the threat of sending me back.

Unlike previous times we've interacted, there's no emotion in his voice. There's no indication we even have a history. It's as if this is parenthetical to all that, and though this is highly personal to him, it's not personal between us. Between us it's professional, impersonal, an exchange of information.

"You're sure?" he says.

"But," I say. "The work she does . . . giving guys a type of girlfriend experience . . Several guys. Every night. That's like . . . multiple affairs on a daily basis."

"That's work."

"It is," I say, "but . . . to be able to do work like that . . . What does that take? She's a good person. She is. And she's not having an affair . . . But if you're this concerned about it . . . why get involved with a woman who does the kind of work she does?"

"I'm already involved," he says. "And if I marry her she won't do that kind of work any longer."

It's beyond bizarre to hear him talking about marriage and seeming to care if his stripper girlfriend is going to be faithful. I first met him while working on a case of a missing teen. She was missing because he had her. He was drugging and raping her and keeping her imprisoned. When I found her with him and saw what he had been doing to her, my rage took over and I beat him so badly he almost didn't survive. He's still not fully recovered and never will be.

"What do you want me to say?" I ask. "I don't think you should marry her. But not because she's havin' an affair."

"If I find out she has been unfaithful to me I will kill her and you."

"Then give me a little more time to double and triple check everything."

I don't need the time but I'd like to stall him as long as I can.

He nods. He still hasn't looked in my direction. "You have a week."

CHAPTER TWENTY-FOUR

AS I APPROACH the old black box truck that houses Mug Shots, Natasha Leone sees me and steps out of the back door and meets me a few feet away from it.

"How's the investigation going?" she asks in her scratchy voice.

"We're making progress."

Three young people are in line at the truck.

The one at the window, a tall, thin African-American woman in her early twenties is ordering a large Under Oath with soy and extra whip and a Citizens Arrest with oat milk and no whip.

The breeze blowing in off the bay causes Natasha's mass of thick, unruly blond hair to cover her face, and she pushes back against it with both hands in a futile attempt to get it under control.

"I just feel so bad," she says. "And want to help in any way I can. Everybody is talkin' about your investigation and some of them seem very scared. Have you uncovered any evidence that proves it either was or wasn't an accident?"

"Most of what we've found so far suggests it wasn't an accident, but we've still got a lot to do. We haven't even interviewed everyone yet."

"I had a thought," she says. "Most of us had to share a bed that night . . . There were so many of us. Those of us who did . . . for lack of a better word . . . have an alibi. Might be a way to narrow down who could've actually done it."

I nod. "That's a great idea."

"I shared a bed with Cherry Lewis. I asked her to come talk to you and she agreed."

"Thank you," I say. "I really appreciate that. That's more helpful than you can imagine."

"She's at a table over in the courtyard," she says. "Want to go speak to her now?"

"Sure."

We walk over to the back of the Taproom and enter the courtyard.

The Taproom is a small pub in a historic building at the corner of Beck and 11th that specializes in craft beer. It's a cool venue with live music and special events and rotating local food trucks in the parking lot.

With a large meeting room and bars both inside and out, the Taproom always has something going. Tonight there will be a band out back and an art show reception in the meeting room.

The courtyard has a stage that runs along the back wall and several seating areas centered around gas fire pits.

We find Cherry Lewis sitting in a chair around the fire pit nearest the parking lot.

"This is Lucas Burke," Natasha says. "Cherry Lewis."

"Nice to meet you," she says and nods.

She doesn't stand or extend her hand, so I just nod back and Natasha and I sit down across from her.

Like Natasha, Cherry is an early-forties white woman. Unlike Natasha, Cherry has shortish dark hair, green eyes, and a high, clear voice that is so soft it borders on child-like.

Cherry owns a gift shop and a restaurant at Pier Park and had a son on the AAU basketball team with Tracy and some of the other women at the party.

"I'll tell you upfront," she says. "I'm only talkin' to you as a favor to Natasha. Tracy's death was an accident like the police concluded and dredging everything up doesn't do anyone any good—especially the family."

"So you don't think it's possible the police made a mistake?" I ask.

She shrugs. "It's . . . I guess it's possible. You think they did?"

"I think they treated it like an accident from the very beginning and didn't really do a thorough investigation. It's possible even if they had they would have arrived at the same conclusion, but we'll never know. They missed a lot."

"So you think one of us killed Tracy?" she says. "That's . . . just . . . nuts. We're not killers. We're not criminals. We're upstanding people. Pillars of the community."

"Upstanding citizens kill people all the time," I say. "But . . . Our investigation has no agenda. Unlike the cops who originally investigated we're not starting out with a theory or belief. We'll follow the evidence. If it was an accident we'll say so—and it will have credibility because it will be after a thorough, unbiased investigation."

"That all sounds good," she says. "But . . . I don't know. Anyway . . . All I can tell you for sure is that Natasha and I didn't do it. We were in the guest room upstairs passed out."

"So y'all were in the guest room," I say. "Do you know where everyone else was?"

Cherry shrugs and looks at Natasha.

"Pretty sure Steve and Adeline were in their room," Natasha ways. "I think Ryan was on the foldout couch in the office in the crow's nest thingy up on the fourth floor. I believe Jamie was in one of the kid's rooms and Tara was in another. Not positive about any of this, though."

"What time did y'all go to bed?" I ask.

She shrugs. "Not sure exactly. Between twelve-thirty and one maybe."

She looks at Natasha for confirmation.

Natasha nods. "That sounds about right."

"And once we did," Cherry says, "we didn't get up again until the next morning."

"How much had you had to drink?" I ask.

"Not as much as the others, but a good deal. More than I usually do, that's for sure."

"Did you do anything besides alcohol?" I ask.

She shrugs. "A little weed and a Xanax . . . I think."

"Did y'all go to sleep right away?"

"Soon as our heads hit the pillows," she says. "We were out."

"And you didn't get up—not even to go to the bathroom?"

"Right."

"Same," Natasha says.

"Okay," I say. "I appreciate it. But you realize all either of you can say is that you went right to sleep and didn't get up until the next morning—because if you did you have no way of knowing what the other person did."

"See?" Cherry says to Natasha. "I told you they're just trying to prove one of us killed her."

"No, he's right," Natasha says. "We can't know for sure what the other did. I didn't really think this through, did I? Although I will say . . . I'm a light sleeper—especially in a strange place—and I would've known if Cherry got up."

CHAPTER TWENTY-FIVE

"HOW LONG WE gonna work this thing for free?" Blade asks.

I shrug.

We are walking down the sidewalk on the east side of Beck in the late afternoon sun slanting in from the west. We are returning from picking up an ice cream for Alana. We had undertaken the errand together so we could talk about the case.

"I knew your ass wasn't gonna give me a straight answer," she says. "I want to know what happened too and I want to get some justice for Tracy's family, but . . . we ain't a charity and we can't function without money coming in."

I am holding Alana's ice cream cone, a colorful swirl polka dotted by even more colorful sprinkles. Blade is working on a cone of her own in-between speaking.

"I know, but we're bucks up right now and—"

"We won't be for long if we stay on a case that doesn't pay."

"Can't really do much while we're waiting to see what Dimitri does."

"We're supposed to be working Kaylee's case," she says.

"I know and we will," I say. "We can work both or you can

work on that while I finish up this one. I'm just not ready to quit this one yet."

"We both know you never will be until it's done."

As we round the corner into my parking lot, Losif is standing there with his hands up.

"Don't shoot," he says. "I'm unarmed. And don't call the cops."

Blade drops her cone, draws her weapon, and points it at him. We both scan the area.

"It's just me."

I pull out my phone and call Ashlynn. "Y'all okay in there?" I ask.

"We're good."

"What's the word?" I ask.

She gives me the correct safe word.

"We're right outside," I say. "Someone's out here. Nobody's inside?"

"Just me, Alana, and Bobby Doll."

"Okay. We'll be inside shortly. Tell Alana we got her ice cream."

"Step over here," I say to Losif.

I nod toward a spot between an oak tree at the edge of the lot and the SUV parked next to it, which will give us some cover if this is a setup.

Blade and I both continue to scan the area as we follow him over to the tree.

Blade stands with her back to the tree. I stand with my back to the vehicle. And we scan different directions as we talk to Losif.

"What're you doin' here?" I ask.

"Cops aren't going to put a wire on me," he says. "They're too small-time. Not enough organized crime in the area. They're not set up for something like this."

I nod. Figured as much.

"I'm gettin' out of town," he says. "And y'all should too.

Dimitri is desperate. He's settling old scores. It's not safe here. And even if you stay in town . . . you don't need to be here where everyone knows where you live. It's not safe. Even with protection. You need to be somewhere you have no connection to. I had hoped to take Dimitri down. Get some justice for Uncle Lev, but . . . can't do it by myself. Don't let him get that little girl. Whatever you do. Don't let him do that."

With his hands still raised, he turns and slowly walks away, down the parking lot, onto the sidewalk, out of view, out of our lives.

"Hey," Blade calls after him, "your ass owes me an ice cream cone."

"Need to get Alana's in to her before it melts any more," I say.

We head toward my apartment.

"Whatcha think?" Blade says.

"I'd feel better about keepin' them somewhere else."

"You think Dimitri's really comin'?"

I shrug.

She says, "Hard to see him still caring about us with all he's dealin' with tryin' to keep the crown."

"Yeah. Maybe. But . . . and I know time is . . . I know it has been a little while, but . . . let's not make the mistake of letting our guard down."

CHAPTER TWENTY-SIX

HAYDEN AND HARPER COOK are twin sisters who own and operate two bakeries in—Bake My Breath Away at the beach and Bake it Stop in town.

It's early the next morning and we're meeting with them at their in-town shop, which is located in a shopping center on the west end of 23rd Street.

I turn my head and stifle a yawn into the top of my fist. We had moved Ashlynn and Alana to a safe house Pete had secured for us in the middle of the night and I hadn't been able to sleep any after that.

We are engulfed in the sweet scents of sugar, cinnamon, vanilla, and the aroma of baking breads and cookies and cakes.

While Blade and I speak to them in the back corner of the enormous kitchen, their college-age kids are operating the front counter.

Even in their mid-forties, the twins are still identical.

They are both thin and stand about five-four with long, straight dark hair, dark eyes, and thick dark eyebrows. As far as I can tell, neither is wearing makeup, and there's a purity and freshness to their faces. They both have a mouthful of large, bright white teeth, which they flash often with their quick smiles.

"We weren't going to talk to you," Hayden says. "And not just because we weren't there and don't have anything to contribute."

"We've tried to stay out of all this," Harper says. "Away from the sick psycho drama."

Hayden says, "But Natasha sells our goodies out of her coffee truck and asked us if we'd reconsider."

"She's one of our best customers," Harper says, "but we're not doing it because we're afraid of losing her business."

"We like and respect her," Hayden says. "If she thinks it's important to do this and it might help in some way . . . then we're doing it."

Their back-and-forth way of speaking and finishing each other's thoughts is so smooth and seamless it's like talking to one person.

"But . . ." Harper says, "that being said . . . we weren't there when it happened."

"And don't know what we have to offer," Hayden adds.

Harper says, "We left early because we have to be here by three in the morning to get everything started."

"We were gone by midnight," Hayden says.

"The others were drunk and as we were leaving they were sayin' 'Time to make the donuts.'"

"We'd like to hear your observations from the time you *were* there," I say.

"It's the last time we've seen most of them," Harper says.

"Did you have a falling-out?" I ask.

Hayden shrugs. "Not per se, but . . . we definitely had our fill of most of them that night."

"Especially Adeline and Steve," Harper says.

"Steve and his friend should've never been there," Hayden says.

"Both of them hit on both of us," Harper says.

"Always wanted to do twins, they said," Hayden adds.

"I mean," Harper says, "it's not like we haven't heard that before, but from the husband of a so-called friend and his friend who weren't even supposed to be there."

"And to be so blunt and bold about it," Hayden says. "It was . . ."

"It made us extremely uncomfortable," Harper adds.

"We called them on it," Hayden says. "In front of the others."

"And all they did was laugh it off and act like it was just a big drunken joke," Harper says. "That's when we left."

"We could've stayed longer if we wanted to," Hayden says. "But if it had happened earlier we would've left earlier."

"It wasn't cute or funny or boys-will-be-boys bullshit," Harper says. "It was aggressive and assaulting."

"They act that way to the other women too?" Blade asks.

They both nod in such unison and with such similarity as to be synchronized swimmers.

"Especially Tracy," Harper says.

Hayden adds, "The most unique or exotic women there that night were a set of twins and a black woman."

"Up until the time you left," I say, "how drunk was Tracy?"

"She was pretty lit," Hayden says.

"She was having a great time," Harper says. "Really enjoying being there. She had a lot of energy. Wanted to party and have a good time. And she kept throwing back the drinks."

"Was she slurring her words? Unsteady on her feet?" I ask.

They shrug in unison.

"Not really," Hayden says.

"Maybe a little," Harper says.

Blade says, "How'd her condition compare with the others?"

"Of the people drinking . . ." Harper says, "she was . . ."

"Right there with them," Hayden says. "Or a little ahead."

"We encouraged her to go home when her husband stopped by," Harper says. "Mostly because of Ryan and Steve. But it was still early and she was having such a good time . . . she wouldn't hear of it."

"Then we tried again when we were leaving," Hayden says. "The party was winding down. The other women were slowing down, some beginning to go to bed. We were hoping she'd go with us."

Harper says, "We offered to give her a ride. Nearly insisted. Practically begged her. Told her one of us could follow the other with her car or she could get it the next day. But she was pretty belligerent by this point."

"It was clear she didn't get out much and wild horses weren't getting her away from there," Hayden says. "Not sure what else we could've done, but . . ."

"Wish we'd've done something," Harper adds.

"When you first heard about it and now since more has come out and you've had time to think about it," I say, "did or do you think it was an accident or . . . something else."

Harper says, "I never for one moment thought it was suicide. Ruled that out right away. Thought then and think now . . . if it was an accident . . . it's one of those bizarre freak accidents that you can never quite explain. Still feels like it's most likely that someone killed her. I don't buy that it was the whole group or that it was planned or calculated."

"Not sayin' whoever did it even meant to," Hayden says, "but . . . they did."

"Who do you think it could've been?" I ask.

"We have no idea," Harper says. "We're not pointing fingers at anyone, but . . . if you say who're some of the most likely . . . You have to start with Ryan and Steve."

It makes sense. It would've taken some strength to get her body up over the railing.

"Then Adeline," Hayden says. "You could tell all Steve's aggressive flirtations was getting to her. Tabitha would be next on our list. She didn't speak to Tracy all night and you could feel the hatred coming off her."

"She's the one who's son lost his starting spot to Tracy's son and then was suspended. She blamed both on Jamal and by extension Tracy."

Hayden says, "Tracy tried to interact with her throughout the night, but Tabitha was having none of it."

"Although," Harper adds, "rumor has it . . . that sometime after we left the two of them got into it and there was an altercation."

Blade says, "Like a fight or some shit?"

"We weren't there," Harper says. "So can't say for sure. But . . ."

"We heard it went beyond just screaming and yelling," Hayden says.

"It may be nothin'," Harper says, "but . . . after his mom died . . . Jamal quit the team and then suddenly . . . Chad was reinstated and got his starting role back."

CHAPTER
TWENTY-SEVEN

WE FIND Chad Meeks shooting basketball by himself on the outdoor courts at Oakland Terrace Park on 11th Street.

Oakland Terrace is a massive 28-acre recreation complex with playgrounds, covered picnic pavilions, gazebos, tennis courts, softball and baseball fields. On weekends it's packed with kids playing, family reunions, birthday parties, and sporting events, and it's routinely used as the gathering place and starting point for the St. Andrews' Christmas and Mardi Gras parades.

Because he has a different last name than his mom, we had no idea that the Chad we were hired to prevent from sharing nude and sexual pictures and videos of his ex-girlfriend is the same Chad who was replaced on the AAU team by Tracy's son, Jamal.

"We sure was hoping to never see your ass again," Blade says.

He drops the ball and holds up his hands.

He looks a little different in daylight than he had in the cover of darkness the first time we had seen him.

He still looks like what he is—a tall, lanky, seventeen-year-old white boy and his thick brown hair still stands up wildly like he just got out of bed—but he somehow appears more childlike and vulnerable.

"I haven't done anything," he says. "I swear. Ask Harley. Check my phone."

He pulls his phone out of the pocket of his black basketball shorts and holds it out to us.

Blade takes it. "Your passcode the same?"

He nods. "Yes, ma'am."

"Check out Chad with the good manners and shit," she says, as she unlocks and scrolls through his phone. "You scared of us, Chad?"

"Yes, ma'am. I am. And . . . I feel bad for what I did."

I say, "That shows good judgement. You might make a decent human being after all."

Blade holds his phone out and he slowly reaches out and takes it, returning it to his pocket.

"We gotta quit meetin' in parks like this," Blade says.

"People're gonna start talkin'," I say.

"Least this time Little Chad's not danglin' about," she says.

It's mid-morning on a Monday. The sky is clear. The sun is bright. The day is cool with very little humidity.

"Why aren't you in school?" I ask.

"Takin' a personal day."

Blade and I both laugh.

"A personal day?" I say.

"Yeah. Just needed some me time."

"Well, sorry to interrupt your *me time*," I say, "but we've got some questions for you."

"You like basketball?" she asks.

He shrugs. "It's okay."

"Aren't you on an AAU team?" I ask.

"Yeah."

"But basketball's just *okay*?"

"It's more my stepdad's thing," he says. "Do it to keep him off my back."

Beyond the tall, leaning, planted palms lining the sidewalk, the traffic on 11th Street is brisk and breezy and blends with the breeze blowing in off the bay.

"Before we go any farther," I say, "I have to ask. How much product do you have to put in your hair to get it to stand up like that?"

He starts to answer as if it's a legit question.

"We heard you lost your starting spot to some black scholarship kid," Blade says. "And then he got your white ass kicked off the team."

He shakes his head. "He had nothing to do with that."

"You're back on the team now?" I say.

He nods.

Blade says, "Back in the starting lineup and shit."

"What happened to the other kid?" I ask.

"He quit."

"Now, why'd he go and do a thing like that?" Blade asks.

"He . . . His mom . . . He lost his mom."

Blade says, "He lost his mom? Maybe he could hire us to find her."

"I meant . . . She died."

"How?" I ask.

He shrugs. "Fell off a balcony at the beach."

"From one of those tall-ass hotels like those drunk spring break fools?" I ask.

"No . . . a . . . mansion."

"Oh," Blade says, "she was that black woman who went to the all white slumber party and got killed."

He's not sure what to say to that.

I say, "Wasn't that some kind of get together for AAU moms?"

"Was your mom there?" Blade asks.

He nods.

"Did she kill that poor woman to get you back on the team?"

He shakes his head. "*What*? No. No way."

"Your mom is Tabitha Hendricks, right?"

He nods again.

"And she *is* one of the suspects, isn't she?"

"I mean . . . I guess, but it was ruled an accident. She just fell off the balcony."

"Actually," I say, "you can't just fall off that balcony."

He looks confused.

"Not without help," Blade says. "Railing is too high."

"Did your mom give Miss Tracy a hand up that night?" I say.

"No. No way. Not for a stupid basketball—"

"She blamed Jamal for you getting kicked off the team, didn't she?"

"No. She knew it was me. And . . . she didn't care. She was . . . glad to not have to go to so many games. She's not all that into it. It's my stepdad who—"

"So she did it to keep him happy and save her marriage?" I ask.

"No, sir. She—"

"What the hell is going on here?"

We turn to see Tabitha Hendricks standing there.

CHAPTER TWENTY-EIGHT

TABITHA HENDRICKS DOESN'T LOOK like she could be Chad's biological mother.

She's short and thickish with a much darker complexion and black curly hair.

She is dressed in semi-casual clothes and looks like a social worker or an elementary school receptionist.

"What do you think you're doin'?" she says. "He's a minor."

"Mom, what're you doin' here?"

"I came to see why you're not in school, and I'm glad I did. You shouldn't be talkin' to them."

"We go way back with Chad," Blade says.

"You know these people?"

He gives a little half-nod-half-shrug acknowledgment.

"How?"

"Doesn't matter," he says.

"Does to me."

"You want to tell her or do you want us to?" I ask.

He looks at his mom with the sad, shy expression of a six-year-old. "When Harley and I broke up . . . I . . . I didn't handle it too good. I . . . I did something stupid."

"How stupid? And why am I just hearin' about this?"

"I . . . I told her . . . I was gonna share pictures and video of her."

"What kind of pictures?"

"Of us doin' stuff."

"Revenge porn?" she says, her voice rising.

"I wasn't gonna do it. I swear. I would never do something like that. I just thought . . . I was mad and . . . I didn't want her to break up with me."

She's shaking her head, her face a sad mask of disappointment. "I raised you better than that," she says.

"I know. I wasn't gonna do it."

"But to even say it," she says. "To threaten her like that."

"I'm sorry, Mama."

"We deleted the material off his phone," I say. "And so far none of the pictures or video have surfaced online or—"

"And they won't," Chad says. "I would never . . . do anything like that. That was all of them. They don't even exist anymore."

"Then why are you here?" she asks.

"You know why," Blade says.

"Tracy," she says with a sigh and shakes her head.

"We were talkin' to Chad about Jamal and the AAU team," I say. "How he got cut and how he got his starting position back."

"Has nothin' to do with Tracy," she says.

"Well . . . yes it does," I say. "It's her son."

"I meant nothin' with what happened to her."

"So if she hadn't been killed Jamal would still have quit the team and Chad would still have been reinstated and put back in the starting lineup?"

"Well . . . no, I'm sure Jamal would still be playing, but Chad would be back on the team. That had nothin' to do with Tracy's death. And she wasn't killed. She had an accident and died."

"Evidence says otherwise, Tabby," Blade says.

"Come on," Tabitha says to Chad. "Get your things. We're leaving."

"Talk to us first," I say.

"Absolutely not."

"Not even as a courtesy for how we kept Chad's assault out of the news?" I say.

"Or," Blade says, "an investment making sure it stays that way."

"Just answer their questions, Mom," Chad says. "They coulda . . . They've been decent with me."

Tabitha looks at Blade. "You sayin' if I don't play ball you're going to leak information about Chad's . . ."

"Is there a reason you don't want to talk to us?" I ask.

"I have nothing to hide if that's what you mean."

"Talk to them, Mom," Chad says. "Get it over with."

"I didn't kill her," she says to us. "No one did. She got drunk off her ass and killed herself. And in the process did a lot of damage for her family and the rest of us."

"We understand there was no love lost between the two of you," Blade says.

"I didn't like her. So what? I don't like you. And I have no plans to kill *you*."

"Why didn't you like her?" I ask.

"She was loud and obnoxious. She had no manners or couth. And she had the biggest chip on her shoulder you've ever seen."

Blade nods, "Sounds like an uppity nigger for sure."

"Don't put words into my mouth. That's not what I'm sayin'. I didn't say anything like that. Do you want me to talk to you or not?"

"We do," I say. "So obviously you interacted with her before the slumber party."

"Just at the games and AAU meetings. I understand cheering for your son. I do it. But constantly yellin' at the refs and the other players. Screamin'. Pitchin' a fit in the bleachers. You make a spectacle of yourself and take away from the game. And she thought Jamal was a lot better than he really was. You should've seen the way she gloated when he took Chad's spot as a starter. I didn't like her. And I didn't pretend to. I'm not fake. But I didn't want her to die. And I didn't want Jamal to quit the team. I actually like him. He's nothin' like his mother."

"Tell us about that night," I say.

"Started out okay," she says. "The energy changed when Tracy got there. And not just for me. I didn't like her and I didn't interact with her much, but I wasn't the only one who noticed. It was like she was trying too hard. Reminded me of amateurs on New Years Eve or Halloween. They're not used to partying so they put too much pressure on the night and try to fit too much in. That was her all the way. And then things got even worse when Steve and Ryan came up and joined us. I think we all drank more because of them—how they were making us feel. I know I did."

"Did you see Ryan hitting on Tracy?" I ask.

She nods. "Him and Steve both. Tracy *and* the twins. It was all kinds of sickening. Felt so bad for Adeline. They were both wasted, but . . ."

"Did you have any interaction with Tracy?"

She shakes her head. "Didn't speak a single word to her the entire night. She tried to talk to me when she first got there but I walked away and started talking to someone else. She didn't try again."

"Real mature, Mom," Chad says.

"She didn't have to gloat the way she did. And I don't have to like everybody. Wait 'til you have kids. You'll see. Somebody messes with your baby . . . you'll . . . You won't want to be their friend either."

"Where did you sleep that night?" I ask.

"In the book nook. There's like a built-in padded bench. I put a pillow and blanket on it and I was out. Didn't wake until the next morning when the body was discovered."

"The body?" Blade says.

"The victim," she says. "Tracy. Look, I'm not gonna stand here and act like I'm broken up about her bein' gone. 'Cause I'm not. Everybody keeps on talkin' about what a tragic accident it was, but . . . something's only tragic when it happens to an innocent. She should've never been drinkin' and druggin' like that. There's one person responsible for her death and it's her. She even had a chance to leave earlier in the evening and she refused it. How can you blame anybody but her?"

"You the one who called her husband?" I ask.

"I didn't call him," she says. "I didn't have his number, but I sent him a message through Messenger."

"'Cause you's all worried about her and shit?" Blade says.

"Nope. 'Cause I wanted her gone. But she was trashed and she needed to go. And what happened to her later that night proves I was right. So . . . as I said. What happened to her was an accident, but . . . it wasn't tragic. It was stupid."

CHAPTER TWENTY-NINE

BRANDY LINTON IS A LARGISH, forty-something white woman with a pronounced Southern accent and blond hair that comes from a bottle. Her carefully applied makeup conceals some of the more obvious signs of aging and her stylish clothes help hide some of her excess weight.

Her carriage and bearing announce her monied importance and remind us just how fortunate we are that she's willing to grant us an audience.

Like a lot of wealthy women with no job and nearly grown kids, she is a prolific and tireless volunteer for good causes in the community.

The cause du jour is local arts.

We meet her downtown on a closed street in front of the Center for the Arts for an interactive arts festival that combines street chalk art installations with live music, art projects, and creative vendors.

We find her standing next to the information booth near the kid's zone where kids and their parents are working on various art projects, most of which involve drawing on 4th Street with sidewalk chalk.

To the left of the information booth is a leather works vendor and to the right is an African-American mermaid artist dressed as a mermaid who happens to be an ex of Blade's.

Her name is Zuri and I wave to her as we walk up. She gives me a small smile and a nod, but avoids eye contact with Blade.

"Isn't this a great event?" Brandy says.

All around us a throng of attendees move about, flitting from street artist to vendor booth like spring bees pollinating wildflowers, all to the soundtrack of a local band playing upbeat covers.

"It's one of my faves," she says. "I love seein' the kids create art alongside the professionals. And we raise a lot of money for local arts programs."

I nod and start to agree with her, but she continues, uninterested if I or anyone else agrees with her.

"Y'all take a moment before you go and make some art," she says. "Promise me you will."

"Blade has made some of the mermaid art before," I say. "I bet she'd like to make some more."

Blade punches me in the shoulder.

The band brings "Listen to the Music" to a close and immediately goes into "You're no Good."

I glance over at Zuri, who is smiling to herself. I knew that would be her reaction to the song. She catches my eye, nods toward Blade and gives me a wry smile.

"Surely that's not your real name, is it?" Brandy says.

Blade shrugs. "It's pretty damn real."

"I . . . I guess I meant your legal name."

"No, ma'am. It's Alix."

Brandy nods her approval. "That's much better. Isn't this just the most beautiful day. It's glorious. Couldn't be better if I'd've special ordered it. Well, I only have a few minutes. As you can see. So what can I do for you?"

"We're taking another look into Tracy Adam's death," I say.

"Why?" she says. "I mean . . . What in the world for?"

"Just to see if anything was missed."

"My word, this thing'll never end, will it? Well, I can tell you . . . I have absolutely nothing to add to what I've already said."

"No need to add anything," I say. "You were the last person to see her that night, right?"

"I felt bad leaving her," she says. "I lingered for a while. Tried to get her to let me give her a ride home. When she wouldn't do that, I tried to get her to go to bed. She said she would turn in after one more smoke. If she had just not . . . If I could've convinced her to let me give her a lift or to go to bed . . . I wish I would've stayed."

"What time did you leave?"

"Around 2:30 I think," she says.

"What state was she in?" I ask.

She looks confused. "What do you mean?"

Blade says, "How fucked up was she?"

I add, "We've been hearing conflicting accounts of exactly how intoxicated Tracy was."

"She was okay," Brandy says. "You could tell she had been drinking, but she wasn't fall-down drunk or anything like that."

"You sure?" I ask.

"Of course, I'm sure. I wouldn't say it if I wasn't. Why?"

"A lot of the people trying to push the accident theory say she was so trashed that she stumbled out onto the balcony, climbed up on the railing and dove off."

"It's not a theory," she says. "However it happened it was an accident, but understand this—she was not fall-down or blackout drunk. I would't have left her alone if she had been."

"Where was she when you left?"

"Finishing up a snack in the kitchen," she says. "No, wait. That's not . . . exactly . . . right. When I said goodbye to her, she was in the kitchen finishing a snack. Sorry. That's when it felt like I left—think I even opened the front door, but I remembered I needed to pee, so I went to the bathroom for a quick pit stop and then I left. It was only a few minutes, but . . . that's what happened. And when I came out of the bathroom and walked to the door, she wasn't in the kitchen anymore. I didn't really think anything about it at the time. I just assumed she had finished her snack and was out back having one last smoke before bed. God, I wish I'd've gone out there to check on her or talk to her until she finished and saw her safely inside. Could've saved her life. I . . . just didn't know."

"Did you see or hear her or anyone else?" I ask.

She shakes her head. "No one. I couldn't even swear she was on the balcony. I'm just guessing that's where she was. That's where she said she'd be. I mean where she was going after her snack. That's it. That's what I told everyone back when it happened and that's what I'm tellin' you now because it's the truth."

"Why didn't you spend the night?" I ask.

"Can't sleep anywhere but my bed," she says. "And I had no desire to share a bed or even a room with . . . any of those women."

"Do you know where Tracy planned to sleep?" I ask.

She shakes her head. "She didn't say. There was no real plan. Everyone just sort of found a place. I'm sure Adeline had everyone assigned to a room, but once she and Steve started fighting . . . She did an Irish goodbye and—"

"What's that?" Blade asks.

"Huh? Oh, when you just sort of disappear—leave without letting anyone know."

"And that's what she did?" I ask.

She nods. "There one moment. Gone the next. Not a word to anyone. I tell you what I wonder . . . Where did Steve sleep? She was seethin'. No way she let him in their room that night."

CHAPTER THIRTY

THE DOOR to my small apartment is ajar, the section around the handle splintered.

I've stopped by to check on the place and grab come more clothes and supplies for the safe house.

I stand to the side, using the wall for cover, wishing I was allowed to carry a weapon.

I ease open the door and look inside.

The place is trashed.

Papers and trash are strewn all about, furniture turned over and smashed, kitchen items in the living room, broken glass, torn and scattered clothes.

And blood.

I rush inside.

It may be an ambush, but I've got to see whose blood it is.

No one should've been here—not with Ashlynn and Alana at the safe house and Pete and Bobby Doll protecting them there.

Did Lexi or Heather drop in at the wrong time and run into Dimitri or Bogdan?

I step as carefully and as quickly as I can around the debris, scanning the living room and kitchen as I do.

Everything I own is secondhand, grabbed in haste from the

dusty shelves of Goodwill, the Salvation Army, and flea markets, but it's still painful to see it in pieces, and it feels like such a violation.

Thinking about Alana being here just a few hours ago fills me with so much anxiety I begin to shake. Of course, that's a result of the adrenaline also.

I take a few slow, deep breaths and try to slow my heart and calm my nerves.

There's a lot of blood. Droplets. Pools. Long, arching strings.

Most of the broken and scattered debris has blood spatter on it.

I make my way over to the bedroom where Ashlynn and and Alana have been sleeping and push the door open.

The bed is overturned. The nightstands are broken. The mirror on the dresser shattered. Blood spatter covers it all as well as the floor, ceiling, and walls.

I'm trampling a crime scene, my shoes making prints in the blood, but it can't be helped.

I move over to the bathroom and open the door.

And find the body.

There slumped on the floor between the toilet and the tub, his head hanging down, is the dead body of Losif Sokolov.

CHAPTER THIRTY-ONE

"IT'S A TWOFER," Blade says. "Take Losif out, send us a message, and set you up."

"That would be a threefer," I say.

After making sure Ashlynn and Alana were okay, I called Blade and Pete.

Blade beat him here.

We're standing in the bedroom looking into the bathroom at Losif.

I say, "Wonder if this was the plan or an improvisation."

"Whatcha mean?"

"Maybe they came here to kill us," I say. "Or kidnap Ashlynn and Alana . . . found nobody home so decided to set me up."

"Lot of fuckin' rage in what he did to him," she says.

I nod. "Intimate too. Up close. Personal."

Losif was stabbed to death, but before he was he had been subjected to countless cuts and slashes.

"Definitely Dimitri," I add.

"We not the only ones he sendin' a message to," she says.

"True. Wonder if he did this on his way out of the country or as a sign he's staying and a warning for anyone else tryin' to take him out."

"Guess we'll soon find out," she says.

"Guess so."

"Still think we should take the fight to him," she says. "You know a bitch be tired of just hanging around waiting."

"We're not just waiting around," I say.

"You know what I mean. Act instead of waiting to react."

"I'm about there. May not have much of a choice—if I go down for this. Definitely do it before I go back inside."

"You don't think Pete and Lexi can get you out of this jam?"

I shrug. "Might keep me from gettin' charged with murder, but . . . probably not from a violation of probation charge."

Pete arrives a few minutes later.

"Jesus, that's a lot of blood," he says as he walks up behind us.

He looks into the bathroom.

"Is that Dimitri Sokolov's cousin?"

"Yeah."

"Is he dead?"

"Pretty sure," I say.

"And y'all didn't have anything to do with it?"

"Nothing," I say.

"True story," Blade says. "We've been working all day. Plenty of upstanding citizens will give us an alibi."

"Okay. We'll need to get those and statements from you and—"

"Can you keep my man out of the big house or not?" she says.

"Should be able to. It helps that I made everyone aware of the situation when I requested the safe house. Will probably still need some help from Lexi."

I nod. "I'll let her know."

Blade says, "It too much to ask for y'all to use this to take Dimitri down for this?"

"We'll certainly try . . . but unless there's any direct physical evidence . . ."

I say, "You'd think doin' this much damage with a knife . . . he'd've left some DNA behind."

"We'll soon find out. Okay, let's get out of the crime scene, get you two out of here, and let me get to work on this."

"Thanks, Pete," I say.

"Don't thank me yet," he says. "See if I can pull it off first."

CHAPTER THIRTY-TWO

ALANA and I are playing Greedy Granny on the floor of the little living room later that night when Lexi arrives.

"You can play with us," Alana says. "Here."

She hands her some of the plastic snacks she's already removed from Granny's tray.

"Thank you," Lexi says, and joins us on the floor.

"You have to take the snacks off her tray without waking her up," Alana says. "If you wake her up . . . she pops up and her false teeth fly out and you lose."

"So don't get greedy like her and take too many snacks," Lexi says. "Got it."

"Well . . . but . . . you have to take how many ever snacks you spin on the card."

"Oh. So I want a low number."

"Yeah. I want Luc to lose."

"Yeah," Lexi says, giving her little fist a bump, "we girls have to stick together. Fight the man."

"Yeah," Alana says. "Fight the man."

We play with Alana for a while, during which time I hug her often, then we put her to bed, which takes a while.

Eventually, Ashlynn turns in also, and it's just the two of us on the stiff, uncomfortable couch.

Whether it's because of how close death came to our door tonight or the threat of being sent back to prison or something else, I feel especially close to Lexi and I want more than anything to be inside her. The safe house is small, but there are two bedrooms, and with Ashlynn and Alana in one of them that leaves one for us.

I'm about to suggest taking advantage of the second bedroom when she says:

"God, my heart breaks for you."

"Why's that?"

"You serious?"

"Just wondering what you mean."

"The way you're living," she says. "Always teetering on the precipice, always about to lose it all. You're so good with Alana and she really needs you, but . . . you could be taken from her at any moment. How long do you think you can go on like this?"

"Want to hear something funny?" I say. "This is about the best my life has ever been. I think I'm doing okay."

"That's why my heart breaks for you."

"I haven't lost it on anyone in a while," I say. "The anger management seems to be helping. I have a family—I mean, all that we're doing is about keeping Alana safe. You're in my life . . ."

She doesn't say anything and we fall silent a moment.

"I'm not sure I can get you out of this," she says. "But even if I can . . . How long before there'll be another situation just like it —or worse?"

She's right. It probably won't be long until I'm right back in a similar predicament.

"Just do different work for the next two years so I can keep you out of prison."

"This has nothing to do with my work," I say. "And everything to do with me trying to stay out of prison. This began because Owens is blackmailing me to do some work for him to keep from going back to prison."

"The thing is . . ." she says, "I . . . I don't think I can do this anymore."

I wonder if she means get me out of jams or be my probation officer or be my friend and sometime lover.

"I care about you," she says. "Deeply. Sometimes it seems more than you care about yourself. I'll still help you all I can, but . . . it hurts too much to . . . It's not like we're in a real relationship anyway, is it? But whatever this is . . . I can't do the sometimes, occasional, part-time, seeing other people, and I can't be with you just to watch you self-destruct."

"You met someone on the dating service, didn't you?" I say.

"I haven't even been on a date yet," she says. "There is no one else. There's just me . . . and my need to protect me."

CHAPTER THIRTY-THREE

THE NEXT MORNING Blade and I are in our office going over the security log from the night of Tracy's death.

I'm distracted and irritable, sleep deprived and wondering what the blowback will be from Losif being found dead at my place.

"Wasn't Lexi with you at the safe house last night?" Blade says.

"Yeah."

"And didn't you get some?" she asks. "Why aren't you in a better mood?"

"She was only there long enough to break up with me."

"Oh. No wonder you all ill and shit."

A few moments later, Luna arrives carrying file folders.

Unlike the previous times we've seen her, her stylish and revealing clothes aren't paint spattered.

"New threads?" Blade says.

"Huh?"

"No paint."

"There will be by this afternoon. Dad got held up but he'll be here soon."

She acts as if she's expected, as if we have an appointment, which we don't.

She glances at the logs on the desk in front of Blade as she sits in the client chair next to me.

"Y'all are going over the security logs," she says. "Good. I have some questions."

"We just started," Blade says, "so we don't have any answers yet."

"Mind if I go over them with you?" she says. "I've studied them a lot."

"Help yourself," Blade says. "Tell us what you know."

Luna opens one of her folders and pulls out the security log. Unlike the ones Blade and I are looking at, hers is marked up with highlighters and annotated with a blue pen.

"Every time an exterior door is opened or closed it is entered into the log," she says. "There are four exterior doors at the house—the front door, the sliding glass doors on the back deck on the second story and the one on the ground floor that goes to the game room, and a side door that opens onto the wraparound decking on the west side. Only three doors registered as being used that night—the front and the two back. The side door wasn't opened at all."

"We're trying to match the door log with what everyone is saying about when they came and went," I say.

"I've done that too—well, as much as I could, and I still have some questions."

"Let's go through it line by line," I say.

She nods. "Okay. Well, I don't know how far back you want to go, but we have the front door opening and closing several times as most of the women arrived for the party between six and seven. We also have the back deck door opening and closing some during that time."

"Probably the ladies checking out the view as they arrived and looked around," I say.

She nods. "That's what I figured. Everybody's pretty much

there by 7:15. And by 7:22 the back sliding glass door is closed for the last time for a while. Then the front door opens and closes again at 8:32, which is around the time Tracy arrived."

"Blade says, "They had all been together for an hour and a half, two hours before she got there."

"Yeah," Luna says, "she cooked dinner for Dad and Jamal and cleaned up before she left."

"So," Blade says, "not only was she the only person of color and the only one not in the same socioeconomic situation as the rest of them, but she came in after they had been partying and drinking and bonding for hours before she got there."

"Exactly," Luna says. "And that's the last time the front door opens and closes for a while. The sliding glass door of the deck opens and closes every half hour or forty-five minutes or so for the rest of the night."

"Which lines up with the witness statements saying Tracy was going out to smoke throughout the night," I say.

"I'm sure they weren't all her, but yeah, that's what they say," Luna says. "Then we have the bottom floor door open and close at 9:06. That's the exterior door of the game room. That's the only time it opens and closes the whole night."

"'Cause they horny asses went upstairs and joined the party," Blade says.

"Yep," Luna says. "Still wish they'd've done a rape kit."

"That the kind of shit that gets skipped when you rule it an accident too early," Blade says.

"The front door opens at 10:27 and closes at 10:32," Luna says. "I think this was the police responded to a noise complaint. That's about the time that was supposed to have happened. Then it opens and closes at 11:03."

I say, "I think that's the time Heather Harrison left."

She nods, and is about to say something when Nate walks in.

I stand and give him my seat, then go around the desk and stand by Blade.

"Sorry I'm late," he says. "Had to go by the bank. We sure

appreciate all y'all are doing and don't want y'all working for free. I was able to get a line of credit for my business. Here's a check to keep you going for a little while longer. It's not much, but hopefully it will be enough to get us to the end."

He hands the check to Blade who places it in the center desk drawer.

Luna says, "We're going over the security logs of the door opens and closes."

"Do you remember what time you went over?" I ask.

"Around 11:30."

Luna says, "We have an open and close at 11:37 and again at 11:46."

He nods. "That sounds right. I tried my best to get her to come home with me, but she seemed to be having a good time. She was definitely buzzed and did not want to leave. I was glad she was having a night out. She didn't get many of those. It was nice to see her so relaxed and . . . free. My main concern was . . . I mean, I wasn't crazy about who she was there with, but my main concern was . . . I just didn't want her deciding later that she wanted to leave and try to drive herself home. The thing is . . . and not too many people know this . . . while she was distracted I got her keys out of her purse and took them with me so she couldn't drive herself. I . . . thought . . . it would keep her from hurting or killing herself on the road . . . I . . . Now I wonder if I should have . . . left them. She may have been safer on the road."

"It's not your fault, Dad," Luna says. "She didn't need to be on the road and her not being had nothing to do with whoever killed her and why."

"She's right," I say. "There's no indication she had any intention to leave and Brandy Linton, the last person we know of to see her alive says she offered her a ride but she wanted to stay."

He nods and looks away, blinking several times.

Luna, perhaps to draw attention away from him or give him

something else to think about continues. "Then at 11:59 it opens and then closes at 12:00."

"That was most likely Hayden and Harper leaving," I say.

"Yep yep," she says. "Had to get to their bakery in a few hours. Then that's it until the strangest one of the night. The front door opens at 2:31 and isn't closed until 2:39 and in between that, the sliding door to the deck opens and closes. It opens at 2:34 and closes for the last time at 2:37."

"I think the front door is Brandy Linton leaving," I say. "She went over and opened it, then went to the bathroom, then closed it when she left. When she was leaving the first time she says Tracy was in the kitchen, but when she came out of the bathroom she wasn't and she believed she had gone out onto the balcony for one last smoke before bed. That lines up with the balcony door opening at 2:34 but wonder why it wasn't closed until two minutes later."

"Could be when she came back in," Blade says. "If she came back in and went upstairs . . . Brandy wouldn't have seen her."

"That fits if she never went off the balcony," I say, "but it's possible that she left the door ajar and noticed it a few minutes later and closed it."

"Only if the impossible accident theory is true," she says.

"If she did come back in," I say, "and was murdered, when was her body taken back outside?"

"The front door opens again at 5:58 and closes at 6:01," Luna says.

"That could be it," Blade says.

"Or it could be Tabitha going to work," I say.

"The front door opens and closes again at 6:12," Luna says.

"That could be when she went to work and the other could've been when the body was moved outside."

I nod. "It's possible. She claims to have discovered the body around six when she went to work."

Blade says, "Don't see how leaving for work out the front door caused her to see Tracy's body in the backyard."

"Yeah," I say. "Doesn't add up. Even if she claims to have looked out her window while getting ready. I don't think her body was visible from anywhere inside the house."

Luna says, "The deck door opens at 6:14 and stays open. The front door opens and closes again at 6:29, 6:42, 7:07, 7:36, and 8:01."

"When the first cops arrived they didn't go through the house," I say. "They walked around the side to the back deck, down the stairs, and out to where Tracy was . . . so none of those were them. They were all the people from the party."

"Whatta you think they were doin'?" Luna asks.

"Cleanin' up evidence," Blade says.

"Maybe," I say. "Or putting things in their vehicles or the trash they didn't want the cops to see."

"Still lots of unanswered questions," Luna says.

"Not for long," Blade says. "We gonna go back at these bitches with another round of questions."

CHAPTER THIRTY-FOUR

"I'M ONLY HERE because of how y'all treated my son," Tabitha Hendricks is saying.

I am back at Steve and Adeline's beach house. I'm meeting Ryan Bowman later to look at the video footage but Courtney let me in early so I could do a walk-through with Tabitha first.

Blade is at the safe house guarding Ashlynn and Alana.

"He lost his head a little over his ex," she says. "It was his first real girlfriend and . . . she was not only a lot more experienced than him . . . he was way more into her than she was him. I appreciate that y'll helped him make a better decision and didn't make it public."

We had actually made the decision for him by taking his phone, but I'm glad she feels like she owes us.

"I wish y'all would do the same with this case," she says. "I'm so ready for it to be over. It was a horrible tragic accident. That's all. And yet just because we attended the same party we're constantly being accused of being responsible somehow."

"Well, we're trying to get to the bottom of everything," I say. "And you being here today helps us with that."

"What else can I tell you?" she asks. "I only have a few minutes."

"What time did you leave the next morning and from which door?" I ask.

"Around six and the front door."

"The log shows the front door opening at 5:58 and closing at 6:01 and then again at 6:12."

She nods.

"Which one was you?" I ask.

She shrugs. "One of them. Not sure which."

"Well, did you go out and close the door behind you or did you leave it open for a few minutes and then close it?"

"Pretty sure I closed it right away," she says.

"What time did you discover the body?" I ask.

She shrugs. "Around six I guess. It was when I got up."

"You see why we're asking," I say. "You're saying you got up, discovered the body, and left for work all around six."

"Well . . . obviously . . . all three weren't at the same time. It took a few minutes, so I must have left at 6:12."

"Can you show us where you were when you discovered the body?" I ask.

She nods and leads us up the stairs to the bedroom on the west side of the third floor.

"I just glanced out the window at the beach when I got up and saw her."

We step over to the window and look out of it.

Because of the height of the window on this floor, the size of the deck on the second floor, and the angle, the spot where the body was found can't be seen from here.

"Come over here and point to where her body was for us," I say.

She steps over, looks out, registers the problem with what she's saying, and points to a vague position out a lot farther than where Tracy's body was."

"The place where her body was found can't be seen from here," I say. "Your statement doesn't add up. Not only does it not make sense that you would leave for work right after finding a dead body, but you couldn't've seen her from here."

"Shit," she says. "Shit. I . . . I didn't have anything to do with anything. And I still think it was an accident."

"But?"

"But . . . I had already left. Didn't know anything about anything. Steve called and told me what had happened and said with his position in the court system he didn't need to be the one to find the body, so asked me to say that I had. So I did. That's it. Nothing sinister. Nothing suspicious."

"Maybe for you," I say, "but . . . it's a different story for him."

CHAPTER THIRTY-FIVE

I WALK Tabitha to her car and wait for Ryan Bowman to arrive.

It's a nice evening, and I remain outside to enjoy it. The wind blowing in off the unseen Gulf behind me is cool and breezy, slashing about as the day fades.

Officially, it's off-season, but PCB is never not busy anymore, and beyond the traffic whipping by on 98, Pier Park is loud and crowded.

I pull my phone out of my pocket to check in with Blade when a patrol vehicle, lights on, zips into the driveway, followed by a black unmarked SUV.

The cop car is neither Panama City Beach Police or Bay County Sheriff's, and I'm unable to make out where it's from before the uniform inside jumps out, gun drawn, and tells me to turn around and lace my fingers together on the back of my head.

After I've done that he yells, "On your knees."

When I've complied with that order, he comes up behind me and cuffs me.

"What's this about?" I ask. "I haven't done anything wrong. I'm waiting here for a meeting. And you have no jurisdiction here."

"Do me a favor and shut the fuck up," he says.

After I'm cuffed, he holsters his weapon, pulls me up, and spins me around—bringing me face-to-face with Mike Reeves.

Reeves is taller than both me and his deputy and I have to look up to make eye contact. His height is enhanced by the heels of his cowboy boots and the gallons of his cowboy hat.

"Pretty sure I told you to stay the hell out of my case," he says. "Don't listen so good, do you?"

"Huh?"

"Funny," he says. "We'll see how many jokes you have once I get you back to my jail."

"I'm in Panama City Beach," I say. "In Bay County. Call either of them out here and see what they have to say."

"You're in my custody now," he says. "And in a short while you'll be in my jurisdiction."

"You're kidnapping me and taking me to your county?"

"That's where you'll commit a number of serious offenses and be arrested before a violent inmate looking at a life sentence shivs you in the shower. Where is that Negress dyke partner of yours?"

"Coming up behind you," I say.

He spins around and reaches for his gun, but stops when he sees she's not there.

"You got me," he says. "I'll give you that."

"Didn't mean right this moment," I say, "just that she will be."

CHAPTER THIRTY-SIX

I'M ALONE in a holding cell in the Palmetto County jail.

It's dark. I'm tired and hungry, and have no idea what time it is.

It's late. I just don't know how late. I'm sleepy, but I won't let myself sleep. I know what's coming.

The holding cell is isolated from all the other cells in the building. It's located up front in a corridor near a couple of interview rooms, and is normally used for inmates being processed in or out of the jail.

I've had plenty of time to think and figure and ruminate and worry and catastrophize.

Are the others okay? Is Alana safe? Will Mike and his men go after them? Will Blade and Pete try to find me and will that leave Ashlynn and Alana more vulnerable?

Will I survive the night?

In many ways I feel like my life is just getting going. I have so much more to do, to learn, to experience.

I don't want to die alone in a holding cell in a corrupt sheriff's backwoods county.

I attempt to meditate and think through some of the steps and slogans of my anger management group.

It helps a little but not much.

I turn my attention to Tracy's case.

I think through what we know and what we still need to find out.

I'm trying to do anything to stay awake so I'll be ready when the attack comes.

I figure it will be in the middle of the night when they think I'm asleep and not ready for it. It's hard to tell but it seems like several hours has gone by. Based on my hunger and fatigue I'm thinking it won't be long.

I stand up and begin to pace around the cell again.

When I hear the door at the end of the hall I quickly lie down on the bunk and pretend to be asleep.

The lights come on.

I'm on my stomach with my head on my arm so I can have my eyes open without them seeing that I do.

The large man rushing toward my cell is an officer not an inmate. And he's alone.

He's clutching a nightstick in his right hand.

Quickly unlocking the cell, he rushes me, raising the nightstick and preparing to strike his first blow.

I lunge off the bunk low and fast and take his legs out, tackling him to the ground.

He hits the ground hard and it takes him a moment to gather himself and adjust to his new reality.

He brings the nightstick up but before he can hit me with it, I grab his wrist with my left hand and begin pounding on his face with the bottom of my right fist.

He lifts his head, which only doubles the blows as his head smashes into the cement floor.

He tries to defend himself with his right hand, but it's ineffective.

He wriggles around and tries to buck me off of him but I stay on top of him and just keep pounding away on his face.

His nose breaks and blood begins to flow out of it.

Eventually, he lets go of the nightstick and attempts to defend himself with both of his hands, but it's too little too late.

His eyes are swollen.

His brain is concussed.

And his nose and mouth are bleeding.

His arms fall to his sides as he loses consciousness.

I keep pounding on him.

When I am able to stop, I stand up, grab his nightstick, place it beneath the thin mattress on my bunk, and then begin to kick him in the ribs.

From down the hall I hear the door open.

Soon the deputy and another correctional officer are at my cell door.

The deputy draws his gun and points it at me. "Back away from him and put your hands on your head."

I do.

While the deputy continues to point his gun at me the correctional officer with him drags his coworker from the cell.

When he has him outside of the cell, the deputy closes and locks the cell door, holsters his weapon and helps the correctional officer carry the wounded man down the hallway.

When they reach the end of the hallway, the lights go out again, and the slam of the door echoes down the corridor.

CHAPTER THIRTY-SEVEN

IT'S MAYBE an hour later when the lights come back on.

I don't pretend to be asleep this time.

I watch as Mike Reeves ambles down the hallway and stands in front of the cell door.

He's still in his beige uniform, cowboy boots and hat.

His massive frame nearly fills the height and width of the door.

He looks sleepy and needs a shave, and his uniform is wrinkled in places, its shirt not tucked in all the way.

"For fuck sake," he says. "That officer was just coming into to roust you and soften you up a bit before some questions and you put him in the hospital."

I don't say anything.

"Feel bad for the bastard," he says, "but I got you now. Got your ass on legit grounds. Attempted murder of a law enforcement officer."

I shake my head. "Nothing legit about any of this. And it was self-defense."

"That's one of the most brutal beatings I've ever seen," he says. "Nobody's gonna buy self-defense." He turns and points to a security camera mounted on the wall near the ceiling out in front of the cell. "Got the whole thing on camera."

"Good," I say. "It'll show me lying down in my bunk when he came in with a nightstick to inflict serious bodily harm onto my person."

"Actually," he says, "that first part of the video got deleted."

I nod.

"But don't worry," he adds, "there's still plenty of the rest. And it got your good side."

"Why're you doin' all this?" I ask.

He doesn't respond.

"You didn't kill her, did you? So who're you covering up for?"

"I'm not lettin' some young punk question me and my investigation."

Could this really just be about control?

"I'm the law. Not you. You're nothin'. And pretty soon you'll be less than nothin'."

"Who let you know where I was?" I ask. "Tabitha or Ryan?"

I'd think it has to be Ryan. Why would Tabitha meet with me and confess if it was just a setup?

Or maybe it was Steve. Maybe she let him know she was meeting with me and he knew she wouldn't be able to keep his secret any longer.

"Or was it Steve?" I ask.

He doesn't give much of a reaction, but it's enough.

"So it was Steve," I say. "Why would you do all this for him? What's he got on you?"

"Get some rest," he says. "You're gonna need it."

He then turns and walks back down the corridor.

Then the lights go off again and the door slams.

CHAPTER THIRTY-EIGHT

WHEN SLEEP COMES it comes hard and deep.

I dream I'm in a cell in a tall tower.

I'm naked and alone. Fatigued and wounded.

Alana is tied to a tree at the bottom of the tower with no one to help her as human traffickers and marauders approach.

I'm powerless to help her.

The life awaiting her is pain and suffering—mental, psychological, sexual, and physical torture and there's nothing I can do.

I scream. I shake the bars. I attempt to break out. I beg and plead for help.

But everything I do is futile.

Suddenly, I'm in bed with Heather Harrison in her condo. There's a hurricane approaching and there are people out on the beach that need our help but I want to finish first. I'm so frustrated and in need of some kind of release, but I feel such pressure to hurry that I'm not sure I can.

"It's okay," Heather says, patting me. "It's okay. Take your time. The storm will wait."

"No, it won't."

"You can't save everybody."

"I know."

"You don't."

"I do."

"You say you do but you don't."

"Come on," I say," let's go get them. We have to hurry before the storm hits."

"What about finishing?"

"It'll have to wait."

Then I'm back in the holding cell in Palmetto County but this time the door is open.

Wake up. Get up. Leave!

A voice inside me is settling at me.

Now! Go while you can.

The hallway door is still locked. I can't get out.

Wake the fuck up! Now.

I rouse myself and turn to see that the cell door really is open.

I jump off my bed and look around.

The lights in the corridor are on but no one is out there.

I'm trying to decide what I should do when I hear the heavy metal door at the end of the hallway open.

I lean out of the cell and peer down the hallway.

Two enormous inmates with prison-made knives in their hands are headed my way.

I try to figure out the moves that will give my best chance of survival.

Spinning around, I reach beneath the mattress and grab the nightstick.

I then rush out into the hallway believing my chances better out there than in the small cell.

"Oh, look, he has a stick. Isn't that cute?" the larger of the two men says.

He has a surprisingly high, soft voice.

The other one, who has a much deeper, more menacing voice says, "I'm gonna take it from him and fuck him with it."

I get down in a defensive position, balancing my weight and lowering my center of gravity, then hold the nightstick in my left hand and let it run down my left forearm to block the initial blows.

They decide to take turns. The one with the high voice goes first.

He rushes me, lifting his shank up over his head and bringing it down in a stabbing motion.

I block it with the nightstick and then punch him with an uppercut to the bottom of his chin that he seems not to even notice.

He then shoves me with both hands and I go stumbling back.

I reset myself and he comes at me again.

This time he swings with his left and when I try to block it, stabs straight out with the knife.

I jump to the side and bring the nightstick down onto his wrist.

I manage to avoid getting stabbed but the blow doesn't cause him to drop the knife.

"Shit, man, give me a turn," the one with the lower voice says.

"You'll get a turn. I'm just playin' around a little first."

"What'd your mom tell you about playin' with your food?"

A black figure behind the low-voiced man catches my eye.

As he comes up behind him he tases him in his fat neck.

The big guy drops the knife and falls to the floor not long after it does.

Two more men in black fatigues and riot gear rush up and do the same thing to the high-voiced man in front of me.

"FDLE," one of them yells. "You're safe."

Once the two men are subdued and carried out, Pete comes down the corridor for me.

"Your call to Blade went through," he says. "She could hear part of your conversation in front of the beach house. She called me. I called FDLE. They were already investigating Reeves. Didn't take much convincing to get them to come in. You okay?"

I nod. "Lot better than I would've been if you'd gotten here just a little later."

"Sorry, but that was about as fast as we could manage."

"You saved my ass," I say. "Thank you."

CHAPTER THIRTY-NINE

"LUCAS," Alana yells when I walk into the safe house.

She runs over to me and I pick her up and swirl her around into a hug.

"Let's play," she says. "Mom and Blade won't play with me."

"I need to talk to him first," Blade says.

"Let me talk to Blade and take a shower and then I'm all yours. Okay?

"Okay. But hurry."

"Come on," Ashlynn says, "let's go get your bath before Uncle Lucas gets his."

Alana brings her arms up and bends her knees into a runner's stance "Uncle Lucas . . . I'm gonna beat you."

"No, you're not," I say.

She takes off toward the bathroom and Ashlynn follows her.

Blade and I are left alone in the small dingy living room with the old, mismatched furniture where before us state's witnesses and criminals had crashed.

"You okay?" Blade asks.

I nod. "Wouldn't be if it weren't for you and Pete."

"I's gonna storm the place, but Pete said he could get you out without us gettin' killed or goin' to prison."

"I appreciate it."

"The fuck was Reeves doin'?"

I shrug. "I wondered too. I asked him, but he didn't offer much."

"He just that out of control or is he covering up somethin'?"

"I think it was partially about control," I say. "Don't think his ego can handle anyone disobeying his direct orders. But I think he was doin' it for Steve Ashby too. Maybe some of the others also."

"Think maybe Steve doesn't want us to see what's on the security footage Ryan was going to show us?"

I shrug again. "Possibly. Won't know until we see it."

"Well, let's pay Ryan a little visit and see it."

I nod. "Sounds good. Right after a shower and some sleep."

When Alana comes into the room a few minutes later, her damp hair wetting the tops of her unicorn pajamas, she says, "Lucas, how long are we gonna have to stay here? It smells and it's no fun. There's nothing to do."

"Hopefully, not too much longer," I say. "Soon we'll get a nice new place close to a park or other fun things to do."

"Yay," she yells.

"Just got to sort out a Russian first," I say.

"How long does that take?"

"Been takin' longer than it should," Blade says. "Much longer than it should."

CHAPTER FORTY

RYAN BOWMAN OPERATES a boxing gym in a rounded rusted corrugated metal World War II era building in Downtown Panama City.

He has created a state-of-the-art facility complete with artisan leather heavy bags, speed bags, gloves, and mitts in one of the coolest buildings in the one of the coolest locations in town.

The contrast between the rustic old metal building and the shiny new equipment is extreme and adds to the dichotic ambiance.

We find Ryan in the front right corner of the building inside the 20 x 20 pro ring. Beyond him, students at various fitness levels are working eight heavy bags, four speed bags, free weights, Peloton Bikes, and Peloton Treads.

He has just finished a high-intensity interval training session with a group of about twelve students, and is cooling down.

All around him, the students are drinking water and unwrapping their hands.

He looks away when he sees us and scans the exits.

"Tell me that big bitch ain't about to do a runner," Blade says.

"Ryan," I yell. "We need a word."

Everyone looks from us to him and back again.

He nods and says something to his students.

Ducking beneath the ropes and climbing down off the ring, he leads us outside, across Luverne, to the shade of some oak trees at the edge of McKenzie Park.

"Bet you thought you'd never see me again, did you?" I say. "Figured I'd die in the Palmetto County jail."

"And his ass almost did," Blade says.

"Makes you an accessory to attempted murder," I say.

He shakes his head. "I didn't have anything to do with that."

"You set me up," I say. "Handed me to them."

"NO," he says. "I . . . I didn't do anything. I was told not to go the beach house that evening. That's it."

"Who told you not to go?" Blade says.

"These are very powerful people," he says. "I . . . I can't . . . cross them."

"It was Steve, right?" I say.

He shakes his head again. "I won't say."

"You can confirm it for us or you can be charged with accessory to attempted murder," I say. "It's up to you."

"All he told me was not to go to the house. That's it."

Blade says, "And bein' his little bitch you did what he said."

"He financed my gym," he says. "I owe him so much. He's my friend. He didn't do anything to that woman. None of us did. We're just trying to move on with our lives."

"Did you lie to us about the video?" I ask.

"No," he says. "It's real. And it proves what I said. I was going to show it to you before . . ."

"Before you were told no to come so a bent sheriff could kidnap me and take me to his jail to have me killed?"

"I didn't know any of that," he says. "I swear."

"We still want to see the video," Blade says.

"Here," he says. "It's right here on my phone. Look"

He pulls out his phone and pulls up the video.

Turning his phone to the side so the video will fill the screen, he angles it toward us, and pushes play.

There's only one camera and one angle. Only an image with no sound.

It captures a very small fraction of the great room and the hallway to the bathroom beyond it.

"This the only camera footage you got?" I ask.

"It's the only one they had. Their system was for shit."

From this angle, you can tell there are people in the living room and you even see part of one pass by occasionally, but for the most part all that can be seen is the empty part of the living room.

Ryan says, "They're on the couches just over here out of view. Want me to fast forward it to the part in the hallway?"

"No," Blade says.

"But you can fast forward it until someone is on the screen," I say.

He does.

Adeline and Tara moving from the kitchen to the living room pass by with drinks. Natasha does the same with coffee. Jamie passes by a few times with drinks.

Eventually, Tracy arrives.

We have a good view of her. Rather than sit with the others, she mostly stands behind the couches near a small table that holds her drinks and smokes.

It's sad to watch.

She appears to try to enter in to whatever is going on with the other women, but mostly seems to be watching and drinking.

She drinks a lot.

She moves around a good bit and dances some. She looks like someone trying to have a good time, and maybe she is, but it's definitely as the person at the party doing her own thing. Everything about the video conveys aloneness, nervousness, and awkwardness.

When the other women pass by on the way to the kitchen or bathroom, she attempts to engage and interact with them, but only a few even pause to respond—Heather and Natasha among them.

"This some sad shit," Blade says.

"Yes it is."

"And," she adds, "suspicious as hell this is the only footage from that night."

Ryan says, "I checked all the cameras feeds myself. They weren't even using the system anymore. It only logged the door opens and closes because it did it automatically."

As we continue to watch, Tracy appears to leave periodically with her smokes, and though she heads in and returns from the direction of the back deck, the image isn't wide enough to show us where she's going.

Then more trips to the kitchen and bathroom by the others and more of Tracy standing alone just outside of what's going on.

And then the men join the party.

Tracy is alone no longer.

At various times Ryan and Steve and both Ryan and Steve are standing near and interacting with Tracy.

Even without the sound, it's clear to see that they're flirting and coming onto her—and occasionally having conflict with each other because of it.

When Tracy walks down the hallway to the bathroom the next time, Ryan follows her.

When she steps out of the bathroom, he's standing there and kisses her.

She pushes him off of her and steps back.

And, as he had said, he lets her. And that's the end of it.

She walks back down the hallway and he goes into the bathroom.

A few minutes later when he rejoins the party he doesn't stand with Tracy any longer.

Because we're only seeing the others for short moments at a time, it's hard to gauge their level of inebriation, but Tracy doesn't seem more intoxicated than anyone else, and I conclude her husband was contacted to come get her because of the attention she was receiving from Steve and Ryan.

When Nate arrives, Tracy is surprised to see him. They embrace and he just stands near her for a while.

Eventually, you can tell he's trying to talk her into leaving with him, but she's having none of it.

As she's making herself another drink, he slips the keys out of her purse, hugs her, and leaves.

Later, there is a parade of women heading upstairs to bed or leaving.

Eventually, we see Tracy and Brandy walk toward the kitchen. About ten minutes later, Brandy passes by briefly headed in the other direction.

We never see either of them again.

"That's it," Ryan says. "I kissed her and I shouldn't have. That's it. And nobody did anything to her."

"Oh, plenty was done to her," Blade says.

"And we can see so little of what's actually going on . . ." I say, "there's no way to tell who did what."

"Well," Ryan says, "all I'm sayin' is what I did and didn't do and this proves it."

"Airdrop that to me," I say, pulling out my phone and holding it out toward him. "I want to watch it again on a bigger screen out of daylight."

He hesitates.

"Accessory," Blade says. "To attempted murder. Work with us and we'll make that go away."

He nods and sends me the video.

"Either of you ever want to lace up the gloves and get in the ring with me," he says, "I'd welcome the chance to spar with you."

"I'm your huckle bearer," Blade says. "But we best do it when the gym is closed. Wouldn't want to embarrass you in front of your students."

CHAPTER FORTY-ONE

"MAYBE IT REALLY WAS AN ACCIDENT," Luna is saying. "If the video backs up what everyone says happened . . ."

Luna had been entering the Panama City Center for the Arts when she spotted us talking to Ryan. She had texted and asked us to stop by before we left the area.

We are standing out in front of the funky, colorful arts building. Nate, who had been working on the landscaping having stopped to join us as well.

"I'm not sure there's enough of it for it to do much of anything," I say. "It does appear to corroborate Ryan Bowman's account of events. Maybe."

Nate says, "I realize Luna is the one who hired you and this is probably for her to say . . . but for me . . . I just want to . . . I want y'all to know that all I care about is the truth. If it was an accident . . . I won't be disappointed or . . . in some ways that'd make me feel better. I just don't want y'all feeling like we'll only be satisfied if you find a killer."

"No, I feel the same way," Luna says. "I mean, I guess I was convinced it was one of those rich assholes, but if it's not . . . I'm with Dad. I'd just like to know."

"We ain't ready to say it was an accident just yet," Blade says.

"But we appreciate what y'all are saying," I add. "We'll take the case to as close to conclusion as we possibly can and go where it leads. It's possible that it'll still be inconclusive even then but we'll give you our opinion based on the case work. In some cases that's the best we can do."

"That's all we can ask," Luna says.

A small group of middle-aged women arrive for a pottery class, hair up, aprons on, clay in hand.

We slide down some, farther away from the front entrance.

"Nate says, "I have to say . . . if it was an accident . . . it'd be a relief. She'd . . . she'll still be gone and it'd still be as tragic, but . . ."

He looks away and blinks back tears.

I nod toward him, though he can't see me. "We get it. As much as we want someone to blame when something like this happens . . . a villain to rest our rage onto . . . it can be a relief for a loved one to not have died as a result of the violent act of another."

Luna looks at her dad. "You think . . . If you think it was an accident and it's too painful to continue . . . we can let it go."

He looks back at her and nods. "It's up to you," he says. "It's not too painful if you want to keep going."

Blade says, "If it was an accident . . . why did Mike Reeves do what he did to Burke?"

Luna nods. "I keep wondering that too. What *was* that?"

"We're not sure exactly," I say.

"Are you okay?" Nate asks.

I nod.

"I feel so bad that that happened," he says. "When Luna told me I was like we need to do something but . . . we weren't sure what."

Luna says, "Hard to see someone doing that if it really was an accident."

Blade nods. "*Uh huh*."

"That's true," I say, "but some men like him just want control and dominance. And feel threatened even when there is none—a least none that's direct."

My phone vibrates in my pocket and I pull it out and glance at it.

It's Lexi.

I send the call to voicemail and return my device to my pocket.

I'll call her back when we're done here.

When she immediately calls again I know I have to take it.

"Excuse me a moment," I say. "I need to take this."

I step several feet away from them and take the call.

"Luc," she says—and in that one word I can tell something's bad wrong. "Listen carefully. Dimitri has me. He wants to meet with you and Blade. I'll give you the address. You're to come unarmed. Just the two of you. If you don't . . . I die. If you contact the authorities . . . I die. If you vary from his instructions in any way . . . I die." She starts crying. "I'm . . . so . . . scared."

CHAPTER FORTY-TWO

"YOUR PRIORITY HAS TO BE ALANA," I say.

Blade and I are racing to the farm warehouse on Overstreet where Dimitri instructed us to go.

Having already sped through Callaway, Parker, and through Tyndall Air Force Base, we're flying down the scenic stretch of Highway 98 east of Mexico Beach.

On either side of us hurricane-damaged pine trees lean in random directions. Occasionally, through a clearing to our right we can see the green waters of the Gulf of Mexico.

"So how we gonna play this?" she says.

"I'll go in alone on foot," I say. "You stay with the car out by the road. We trade me for Lexi. I tell him once she gets out there to you, you'll come in, but instead y'all get the fuck out of there and don't look back."

"And leave you to get killed by Dimitri? The hell kind of plan is that?"

"Only one I can think of right now," I say. "But we should also call Bobby Doll and Pete to get them headed out this way so they can clean up the mess if it goes tits up."

"Already done. Texted them a while back."

"Good. I just didn't want them getting out here too soon."

As we cruise through Mexico Beach I look out at the glass-like Gulf as if for the last time, taking in the extraordinary beauty and calm.

When we take a left on Overstreet, I kick it and in a matter of minutes we're atop the high bridge over the Intercoastal Waterway.

"I ain't about lettin' you get killed today," she says. "Lexi ain't worth it."

"I got her into this," I say. "I have to try to get her out."

"You gonna trade your life for hers?"

"If I have to, but maybe it won't come to that. What I'm not willin' to do is trade your life for hers or risk Alana's, so I need you to stay away."

"We take Dimitri out and we all be safe."

A few minutes later, we arrive at the enormous sod farm—hundreds and hundreds of acres in every direction.

I turn onto the narrow dirt road and stop the car.

Putting it in park, I turn to Blade. "I don't say it enough, but . . . I love you. You've been the only family I've ever had and—"

"Hey," she says, sniffling, "if you really mean it live through this shit and tell me afterwards."

"Please stay out here," I say. "Stay alive and protect Alana."

"Least take one of my blades," she says.

I shake my head. "They'll pat me down."

"'Less they shoot you on sight."

I grab her hand, squeeze it, then without another word, jump out of the car and began to walk toward the warehouse.

The corrugated tin building warehouse is a couple of hundred yards down the dirt road.

As I near it, I see that inside and spilling out of it are wooden pallets, some of which still have soil and random chunks of sod on them.

When I reach the large opening of the warehouse I raise my hands and walk inside.

CHAPTER FORTY-THREE

"HEY GUY, YOU CAME," Dimitri says. "Zat's good. Zat's wery good. But you were supposed to bring zeee nigger knifer wiz you."

Standing in front of a large Massey Ferguson tractor with a double finishing mower on the back of it, Dimitri is behind Lexi who is cuffed, and Bogdan is a few feet away from them, holding a semi-auto handgun that looks to be a .9mm or a .45. It's probably a .45.

Dimitri is a lean muscular man with closely cropped hair in his late twenties or early thirties. He's wearing an expensive black suit with a black silk shirt unbuttoned halfway down his chest. Bogdan is an enormous man of around the same age and is wearing an Adidas black tracksuit with three white stripes on the sides of the arms and legs.

"She's right outside," I say. "You have me. Send Lexi out and Blade will come in."

Lexi's head hangs down and her hair obscures much of her face. I've yet to make eye contact wit her. It doesn't appear Dimitri has a weapon on her, just holding her cuffs with his left fist.

"Sure, guy, I vill just send zis blond bitch right out. Let me get on zat."

Dimitri speaks with a heavy Russian accent—replacing i with ee, randomly omitting the articles a and the, rolling his r's, harshing his h's, softening his e's, and replacing his th's with z's and his w's with v's.

"She has nothing to do with this," I say. "You wanted us. You got us. You don't want the heat from fuckin' with a law enforcement officer. Let her go and let's get on with our business."

"But she ees my business now, guy," he says. "From the moment I fuck her tight little pussy. I think I might be in love. No way I let her go. I'm takin' her to Russia wiz me. Make her American-Russian princess. For a little vile anyway. Know what I mean, guy. And yes, guy, I know you vill miss me, but I am going back to Russia. I . . . honestly could not decide what I vas going to do. I thought about just cutting you two—scaring you the way your nigger did us. Leave you alive to walk around wiz my mark. But zee way you disrespect me like zis, only you coming in, telling me to send out my new tight pussy princess makes me just want to have Bogdan off you right now."

"Do you ever plan to come back?" I ask.

"Of course."

"Then why make that more difficult on yourself? You off us and all you do is increase the heat. Our cop and criminal friends will hunt you down and square it. But if you just mark us, you make us your little bitches . . . there's no heat. You can come back and run the city."

He seems to consider it. "One zing is for true . . . Ones vay or anozer . . . You got to pay zee piper, no?"

"I'll pay," I say. "Let her go and I won't resist. You can mark me up or put me down."

"Vat do you say, tight pussy princess?" he asks Lexi. "Do you vant to leave your Russian sugar daddy, huh?"

As Lexi lifts her head slightly I can see that her mouth it taped and she has been beaten up pretty badly.

I can feel the rage rising in me.

I try to calm myself with my breathing.

Dimitri says, "She has had real man now. She von't vant to go back to leettle limp deeck American. Zat is punishment enough for you, my friend. But I vill still cut you up. Come over here. Let Bogdan pat you down."

I walk over to Bogdan with my hands up and he pats me down.

He then shoves me in the direction of Dimitri.

Dimitri lets go of Lexi's cuffs and she falls to the ground.

"If he moves or makes a sound," Dimitri says, "shoot her in zee face."

As Dimitri withdraws a knife from his suit coat and snaps it open I see Blade sneaking up behind Bogdan out of the corner of my eye.

"I vill start with your face, guy," Dimitri says, as he approaches me. "EEf you make peep Bogdan will shoot tight pussy American princess, understand?"

"I under—" I say and nod, but without finishing I lunge at him, my fury taking over.

Grabbing the wrist of the hand that's holding the knife with both my hands I turn it up and stab him beneath the chin with it.

I then tackle him to the ground and begin to pummel him with both fists.

A shot rings out behind me and I realize I've gone too soon. I didn't give Blade enough time to get into place.

Since it was just the one shot I hope it missed and was as Blade was slicing him open, but I'm in no condition to do anything at the moment but beat the fuck out of Dimitri.

I think about him bragging about raping Lexi. I recall his threats to do the same to Ashlynn and even Alana and can't stop hitting him.

Eventually, when I'm able to stop hitting him, I pull the knife out of his chin and begin plunging it into his heart, chest, and abdomen.

"Burke," Blade is yelling. "Burke. He's gone. Come on. We gotta get Lexi to the hospital."

I turn to see Bogdan lying on the ground, his gun still in his hand. His throat is slit and his femoral artery is sliced and he's bleeding out, Blade's precise, surgical strikes a vivid contrast to the mess I've just made of Dimitri.

I glance over at Lexi. Her shirt is covered with blood.

I climb off Dimitri and rush over to her.

"I went too soon," I say. "I should've waited a little longer for you to get in place."

Lifting her, I begin to run with her toward the car.

"I'll run ahead and get the car," Blade says. "Come back and get y'all. I've got an ambulance coming, but they're in Port St. Joe. We'll take her to meet them along the way."

She takes off in a dead sprint for the car.

I continue at a slower pace, stumbling down the dirt road, Lexi's blood mixing with Dimitri's on my shirt.

As I do, I talk to Lexi and try to discern any signs of life, but she feels like deadweight in my arms.

CHAPTER FORTY-FOUR

WE ARE in the emergency waiting room at Sacred Heart in Port St. Joe.

Waiting.

I have washed my face, hands, and arms, but my clothes are still damp with Dimitri and Lexi's blood.

The coagulating blood is causing my shirt and pants to stiffen and crack when I move.

It disturbs me deeply that their blood is mixing, and when I think about him raping her I want to kill him all over again.

Blade, who has remained close to me, is just outside on the phone, pacing around near the window not far from me.

I keep wondering if the cops are about to roll up and arrest us.

I feel a mixture of anxiety and worry and anger over Lexi, what she went through and the low chances she'll survive, but I also feel relief for Alana and a sense of peace at the threat of Dimitri being over.

When Blade walks back in Pete is with her.

I stand and the three of us walk over to the corner of the waiting room for privacy.

"How are you?" he asks me.

I shrug.

"How is Lexi?"

I shake my head. "Doesn't look good. Waiting for an update from the surgeon."

He nods and frowns and says, "So sorry."

"What's happening at the scene?" Blade asks.

"Being processed by FDLE CSI," he says. "It's in Gulf County so it's their case, but we've been assisting since we've been working Sokolov for a while." He shakes his head and considers us. "I could tell immediately which one of y'all did which Russian." He looks at me. "You made a mess of Dimitri. And look at Blade . . . not a drop of blood on her."

"What're we look at for it?" Blade asks.

"Sheriff's Investigator named John Jordan is in charge. He'll be coming to interview you soon. He's a good man and a great investigator. I've explained everything to him. I'm pushing for self-defense. The mess Burke made makes it a little more challenging . . . but the fact that they kidnapped and shot a law enforcement officer helps."

The double doors open and the surgeon walks out looking for us.

His green scrubs have blood spattered on them.

I turn and walk toward him, Blade and Pete following.

He shakes his head. "We've done all we can do. She's being life-flighted to Tallahassee. If she survives the night . . . she might make it."

CHAPTER FORTY-FIVE

JOHN JORDAN IS A TALL, trim middle-aged man with brown hair and eyes who looks about a decade younger than he really is.

He's an investigator with the Gulf County Sheriff's Office.

We're meeting with him in the parking lot near our vehicle at Sacred Heart. Pete is still with us.

Evening is coming on and it's turning colder. The last of the setting sun is fiery orange glow along the eastern horizon just above the tops of the tall pine trees.

John Jordan's kindness as a human being and confidence as an investigator has a calming effect on us.

"Pete has given me most of the background and details," he says. "Could you just take me through what happened today and I'll let you get home and get cleaned up."

I start with the phone call from Lexi and we take him through our actions and thinking that led to this afternoon's events.

Blade fills in various details along the way.

"He said if we involved the authorities he'd kill her," I say, "but we wanted y'all to know in case things went wrong out there so we called when we got close."

"And you were in there alone with them?" he asks.

I nod.

"Unarmed?"

I nod again. "I'm on probation and not permitted to carry a weapon of any kind."

"The big guy . . . Bogdan . . . had a gun and Dimitri had a knife?"

"Dimitri didn't pull the knife out until after we had been talking a while, but yes, it was his. Bogdan had his weapon out and pointed at me the entire time until Dimitri pulled the knife on me, then Bogdan pointed his weapon at Lexi."

"And Lexi is your probation officer," he says.

I nod.

"Any idea why he took her?"

Blade says, "Couldn't get to any of the rest of us."

"But your probation officer?"

I don't respond except to give a small shrug.

"Do you two have a personal relationship?"

I nod slowly. For some reason I feel like I can trust him.

Pete says, "She has helped us guard the little girl Dimitri threatened that I told you about."

Blade says, "She's become a friend to us all."

He nods. "I appreciate your honesty. Your attack on Dimitri seems excessive. Was it because he had taken Lexi?"

"It was because I was unarmed and there were two of them with a gun and a knife," I say. "Just wanted to make sure he wasn't able to hurt Lexi or me."

He looks at Blade, "And you came in while they were fighting?"

"If I had been just a little sooner and Lexi wouldn't have been shot."

"And you had a gun and a knife?"

She nods. "A gun and several knives."

"And you used the knife because . . ."

"I prefer blades."

"You're certainly surgical with them."

I say, "We did the best we could under the circumstances. Wish we could've saved Lexi and kept the two Russian mobsters alive to face prosecution, but . . ."

"I believe part of that statement," he says. "Don't doubt you wish you could've kept Lexi from getting shot."

CHAPTER FORTY-SIX

WE ARE HOME.

We are safe.

My little apartment has been professionally cleaned and fully repaired. There's new carpet, some new furniture, a fresh coat of paint.

It doesn't yet smell like home—the carpet dye and fresh paint overpower every other aroma—but it mostly looks and feels like home, and I'm so glad to have Alana out of the safe house and back here.

We're sitting at the kitchen table, she in my lap, drawing and coloring, our canvases all purpose printer paper.

I hug her often, which she mostly sees as a hindrance to her creative endeavor and shrugs off.

"You are so loved," I whisper in her little ear. "So very safe."

"*Draw, Luc,*" she says, her voice full of exasperation. "Stop talking and hugging and *draw*."

"Yes, ma'am."

I'm a mixed-up mess of conflicting emotions.

I'm worried about going back to prison. I'm worried Lexi won't survive the night, and I'm wracked with guilt over what happened to her. Dimitri taking her and beating and raping her is solely because of her connection to me. And her getting shot is only because I made my move too soon. But I'm also relieved Dimitri is no longer a threat and happy to be back home with Ashlynn and Alana.

The front door opens and Ashlynn walks in with Thai takeout.

"Sorry I took so long," she says, "but it felt so good to be free I just walked around for a while."

"I'm glad you did," I say.

"You starving?" she asks.

"Haven't even thought about it," I say. "Very happy to be right here doing this."

She places the bags on the counter and sits at the other end of the table.

"It's just starting to hit me that I have my life back," she says. "I can go back to work. We can get our own place again and get out of your hair."

"I like having y'all here," I say. "Wish you'd stay."

"You can't keep sleepin' on the couch," she says. "We can't keep living like guests. You've been . . . so amazing. But this place is way too small."

"What if we get a bigger place together?" I say. "Built-in babysitting and we could afford more."

"*Lu-uc,*" Alana says, dragging it out, "I'm not a baby. And less talky talky and more drawy drawy."

"Are you sure?" Ashlynn says. "You'd want that extra—"

"Absolutely positive."

"Well . . . then . . . let's start lookin' for a new place."

CHAPTER FORTY-SEVEN

"SORRY I LET LEXI GET SHOT," Blade is saying.

"You didn't," I say. "I did. I went too soon. Didn't give you time to get in place. It's completely on me."

We are sitting on my couch, sipping some whiskey. It's late. Ashlynn and Alana are asleep in the bedroom, the door closed.

It's quiet and our voices are soft and dry. Alexa is shuffling Bob Dylan songs so low it's barely perceptible. I can only make out bits and pieces of "Girl from the North Country."

"Any word on how she's doing?" she asks.

I shake my head. "No update yet."

"Smells like a showroom in here," she says. "Got that *new* new smell."

"Beats hell out of the wet copper odor of blood and the foul stench of dissected bowel," I say.

She shrugs. "I don't know . . . the smell of dead Russian gangster is growin' on me."

We are silent a moment, sipping our whiskey.

I can make out part of a couple of phrases from "Don't Think Twice, It's All Right."

"I'm beginning to think we've taken the Tracy Adams thing about as far as we can," she says. "Don't want to give up, but . . .

not sure how much more we can do and how much good it will do. What?"

Evidently, I'm making an expression. I shrug. "I don't know. I think you're probably right, but . . . there was something . . . I had the slightest wriggle of an idea when we were watching the video or goin' over the security logs or to a dream I had when I was in Mike Reeve's holding cell."

"Well, what is it?"

I shake my head. "Can't remember."

"Think."

"Yeah, that's not gonna help," I say. "If I ever get it back it'll be when I'm thinking of something else—or nothing at all."

"Well, do that."

I laugh.

"I'm serious."

"Let me sleep on it," I say, "and let's talk about it in the morning. It may've been nothing. If I can't get it back we'll put this case on pause and start working on Kaylee's."

"Deal," she says. "Now stop drinking and start remembering."

CHAPTER FORTY-EIGHT

THE NEXT MORNING I meet Heather Harrison at a popular breakfast spot on the beach called The Early Birdie.

Part bakery part breakfast boutique, the place is always packed.

We're at a small table near the door—the only one available.

All around us people are eating and talking, enveloped in the sweet aroma of freshly baked pastries and the smoky smell of sizzling bacon.

As always, a large number of the patrons present this morning are still in their pajamas.

Though I have no appetite, I have an order of extra crispy bacon and an apple fritter on a plate in front of me.

"How are you?" Heather asks.

I shrug. "I'm okay."

The truth is I haven't slept, haven't been able to remember what I was trying to about Tracy's case, and haven't been able to stop worrying about Lexi and feeling guilty about what happened to her.

"Any word on how Lexi is doing?"

I shake my head. "Not yet. Don't even know if she's still

alive. I'm not allowed to go see her or get any info. Have to get it in roundabout ways."

"I'm worried about you," she says.

I nod. "That's probably not a bad idea."

"I think about what you did . . . And yes you saved Lexi and you destroyed the monsters threatening little Lana, but . . . at what cost to you?"

I pause a moment before responding. "I try not to think about it."

"I bet."

All around us people in pajamas who have never killed a man with their bare hands are enjoying their breakfasts.

"What goes on inside of you when you . . . when that happens?"

"No idea," I say, shaking my head. "Nothing conscious."

"It's a . . . you enter a . . . dissociative state?"

I shrug. "Guess so."

"How you feel afterwards?"

"Right afterwards or like now afterwards?"

"Now afterwards?"

"Like I really want to talk about it," I say with a smile.

"Sorry. I'm just worried about you. Don't know what to do, so I decided to buy you breakfast and ask you a lot of annoying questions."

I shake my head. "Not annoying. I just don't have much in the way of answers. But I appreciate the concern. I really do."

"Are you talking to someone?" she asks.

"You mean a professional? Yes. He's just not very good."

"Then find another one," she says. "Don't stop looking until you find a good one."

I nod. "I need to."

"Let me know how I can help."

"I'm also going to anger management meetings and a rageaholic twelve steps group. And obviously they're working wonders."

"Well, they may be helping more than you know. Just don't stop."

"I need to go," I say.

The truth is I feel guilty sitting here with her while Lexi is fighting for her life in the hospital.

"Sure, of course. Thanks for meeting me. And I'm sorry I'm so . . . It truly is just concern."

CHAPTER FORTY-NINE

"PLEASE, NO," Luna says. "Y'all can't quit."

"We're not quitting," I say. "We're just letting you know we're not sure how much farther we can take the case."

"We're sorry," Blade says. "We really are, but—and we'll still work it as we can—but . . . without more cooperation from those involved . . ."

"Please," she says again.

"If the original investigation would've been better . . ." I say.

She says, "But the fact that Mike Reeves kidnapped you proves they have something to hide and you're getting close."

Nate says, "It really did seem that way."

"Could just be his corruption or a sloppy investigation," Blade says. "But even if it was because one or more of 'em are guilty without the others cooperating . . . we can't . . . get anywhere."

I say, "And the fact that the video corroborates what everyone said . . ."

"But," Luna says, "didn't you say it only showed one little area of the room?"

I nod. "I did. That's true."

"The fact that none of the other cameras worked that night is suspicious itself," she says.

"Oh, they's plenty that's suspicious," Blade says. "We ain't sayin' there ain't. But suspicious by itself don't get us anywhere."

"Please don't give up," she says. "Please."

"We're not," I say.

"Sure sounds like you are," she says. "And if you do . . . it's gonna go unsolved. No one else is working on it. No one else ever will. You know the cops aren't going to."

"We've got a friend on the force who's going to continue to investigate it," I say. "And we're going to also. We have other cases that are ongoing. Some cases take longer than others. We haven't given up on any of those."

"Maybe not, but how much are you really working on them?"

I nod and give her an expression that concedes the point. "Not a lot."

"Just a little longer," she says. "Please."

"We're sorry," Blade says. "We know this wasn't the result you were—"

"What if we try to get everyone together?" I say.

"Huh?"

"In the house. Invite everyone to do a walk through and see what happens."

"They won't come," Blade says.

"We know some will," I say, "and that might be enough to make all or most of them because they don't want to look guilty."

She shrugs. "Might."

"Sometimes getting a group like this one together and talking can shake things lose," I say to Luna and Nate.

"Yes," Luna says. "That'd be great."

I look at Blade. She shrugs again and then nods.

"But," she says, "unless something significant shakes loose for us to follow up on . . . this'll have to be the last thing we do. Okay?"

CHAPTER FIFTY

TWO NIGHTS LATER, we are gathered at the beach house. To my surprise everyone is here.

We are in the main living room area, and nearly everyone is approximately where they were the night of Tracy's death.

Adeline Ashby is on the large leather couch facing east. Jamie Hodgins, Cherry Lewis, Tara Barnes, and Tabitha Hendricks surrounding her.

Hayden and Harper are on the couch next to them that faces west. They are joined by Natasha Leone, and Brandy Linton.

Candi Tucker is standing next to Ryan on the far side of the room near the back sliding glass doors.

Steve Ashby is standing near the kitchen.

Luna is standing where Tracy had been. Nate is beside her.

Blade and Heather Harrison are standing in the entryway where the foyer and the living room meet.

A few others are scattered throughout, including Pete, who is dressed casually and unbeknownst to the others, is here officially.

"We really appreciate you coming tonight," I say.

I'm standing in front of the fireplace and the huge TV mounted above it, which is off.

I am weary and still partially in shock. Still racked with guilt. Lexi is on life-support and is unlikely to survive.

"Didn't really have a choice, did we?" Jamie says. "Would've looked guilty if we hadn't."

She sounds like she has been drinking a good bit before she got here.

"They're so many unanswered questions in this case," I say. "Or at least questions with unsatisfactory answers. How did Tracy actually die? What killed her? Was someone involved?"

"Do you know?" Jamie asks.

On the drive out here I had remembered what I had been thinking earlier and as we got closer and closer I began to see more and more clearly what really happened. It was in the little details of the security log, the psychological makeup of those involved, and the injuries Tracy sustained.

I have little hope for any kind of justice from our legal system —I can't really prove my theory—so this is the best I can hope, getting everyone together, revealing what I think happened, and see how they respond.

"The cops said it was a fall from the balcony," I continue.

"Because it was," Steve says.

"But it doesn't seem possible that she could've sustained the injuries she did from merely falling the fifteen feet or so from the back deck onto the sand below. They also say it was an accident, but . . . the deck railing is too high for her to have accidentally fallen over it. So how did she actually die? Was anyone else involved? If it was some kind of freak accident or a suicide how could it have actually happened?"

Luna says, "It wasn't an accident and she didn't commit suicide."

Ryan says, "We know y'all are sad and all but accusing us of killing her won't bring her back."

"Or," Steve adds, "make y'all less sad."

"Bringing you cocky, entitled assholes to justice will make me a lot less sad," she says.

"See?" Steve says to me. "See what we're dealing with? You can't reason with someone like that and don't fool yourself that they're lookin' for the truth . . . 'Cause they're not. They're just looking for someone to blame. And you're helping them. They're resentful because we have a little money, well guess what? Our family worked our asses off for every dime we ever earned."

"Save it," Adeline says without looking at him. "Poor little rich boy."

"Fuck it," Steve says, "I'm out of here."

He crosses the living room. When he reaches the edge of the foyer, Blade steps in front of him.

"Stay just a few more minutes," she says. "We won't keep you too much longer."

He starts to say something or step around her, but makes a wise calculation and does neither.

"Fine," he says. "Just control your yappin' little bi—female puppy and get on with it."

As he walks back to where he had been, I say, "According to her statement . . . Brandy was the last person we know of to see Tracy alive and she left around 2:30 Tracy was in the kitchen eating a snack. But Brandy didn't leave right away. She intended to. She even opened the front door, but then she realized she needed to go to the bathroom before she left. And as she inadvertently left the front door open as she did. We know this from the security log. When Brandy came out of the bathroom she noticed the kitchen was empty and she assumed that Tracy had finished her snack and gone out back to smoke."

Brandy says, "It's the truth. I mean, it's what I thought. Is that not what happened?"

"I'm not saying she wasn't out there," I say. "But what if someone else was out there with her?"

"Was there?" Jamie asks. "Who?"

"Yeah, who?" Natasha says.

"Someone who came in while the front door was open and Brandy was in the bathroom," I say.

"Really?" Heather asks. "Who? And why?"

"You saying one of us who left early . . ." Hayden says.

"Came back later and killed her?" Harper adds.

"I'll get to which one of y'all did it in a minute," I say, "but first I want to go back to how it was done. See, I think Tracy did die from a fall. It just wasn't from the back of the balcony onto the sand."

"So where?" Jamie says. "Tell us already."

"I think she fell down the metal stairs at the side of the deck onto the cement pad below," I say.

"So it was an accident," Steve says.

"Not necessarily," I say, "but we'll get to that. Falling down the stairs would explain her injuries—the contusions, the bruising, the blunt force trauma. Especially if she went down with some force, which I think she did."

"What does that mean?" Luna asks.

"I don't think she just fell. I think she was pushed—or fell during an altercation."

"So it was murder," she says.

I nod, "By moving her body . . . the killer confused everyone and caused the initial investigators to rule it an accidental death from falling from a balcony that wasn't high enough to cause her death—especially since they claimed she fell onto the sand."

"Heather says, "So it was a fall, but not from where they said and not without some help."

I nod again. Slowly. Deliberately.

For just a moment everyone is quiet and only the hum of the refrigerator motor and the central unit can be heard. The house is so well insulated the sounds of wind and waves from outside can't be made out, which is probably why no one but Tara heard anything. And she only did because she was in the game room.

"So who was it?" Ryan asks. "Who did it?"

I turn toward Nate Adams. "You didn't come back to kill her, did you? You just really wanted her to come home with you."

Luna turns toward him, her tortured face a question she doesn't want an answer to. "*Dad?*"

Her voice is so small, so soft and childlike.

He bursts into tears.

"*No*," Luna says. "*No*."

"I just wanted her away from these . . ."

"These what?" Ryan says. "You're the fuckin'—"

"You murdering bastard," Jamie says to him.

"We've been living under a cloud of suspicion all this time," Brandy says.

"Gettin' death threats," Tabitha says. "Everybody accusin' us of bein' racists murders."

"She wasn't one of them," Nate continues to Luna as if the others hadn't spoken. "And they'd never let her be. She was their maid. I could tell . . . they were laughing at not with her. She wanted so bad to fit in, to gain their approval. It made me sick. It was pathetic. And her drinking only made it worse."

Luna says, "All this time . . . and it was you. *You*. You let me . . . work on this so long and hard . . . and hire these . . . detectives . . . and all the time it was . . . you. *You*."

"I was just trying to take care of her," he says.

"Blade says, "You's tryin' to control her."

"I finally put my foot down with her. I had to. She was making a mockery out of me, out of us, out of herself. I was so patient with her. It's so hard to talk to a drunk, to get them to see reason. I was . . . so patient. She was so . . . belligerent . . . belittling and abusive. I put up with it for a long time, but eventually I had had enough. I didn't mean to hurt her. I just grabbed her by the arm and told her we were going. I pulled her over toward the backstairs. I didn't want to go back in the house. She fought me the whole way. Hitting me. Scratching me. Cussin' me like a dog. I was calm at first but eventually she got to me. I couldn't take it anymore. I was just so . . . humiliated and . . . mad. I was furious. The things she was saying to me. I just . . . I . . . I couldn't . . . I just lost it. When I got her close to the stairs I just sort of slung her toward them. I didn't think she was going to . . . that it would kill her."

"Probably didn't right away," Blade says.

"It was an accident," he says.

"No," I say. "It wasn't. In that moment you may not have meant to kill her, but you threw her down the stairs."

"Dad, he's right. That wasn't an accident."

"I didn't mean to kill her. I just lost it. I had had it with her trying to fit in with these fucks who thought she was beneath them. Made me think *she* thought she really was beneath them, that they were worth all the groveling and humiliation."

"Dad," Luna says again, her voice small and wounded. *"You."*

"I'm so sorry, baby girl. I was really hopin' you'd . . . let it go. But you kept on pushin' and pushin'. Even when they tried to stop . . . you wouldn't let them."

"I thought . . . I was tryin' to get justice for Tracy. I thought one of *them* had done it."

"They did do it," he says. "Don't you see? It's on them. She should've never been here. They should've never treated her the way they did. If they hadn't been such . . . And if she hadn't been drinking so much . . ."

"Dad," Luna says again, the word suffused with hurt. "You're blaming the victim."

"But—"

"Dad," she says, more firmly this time. "Tracy isn't to blame. Neither is . . . anyone else. *You. You* . . . did this. *You* . . . are to blame. *You* . . . killed her. *You."*

Nate breaks down again, dropping his head into his hands, and begins to sob.

CHAPTER FIFTY-ONE

THE FOLLOWING morning is cool and clear, the crisp air brisk and easy to breathe.

Blade and I have just stepped out of the Downtown Boxing Club, where she outboxed Ryan Bowman in a six-round exhibition match in an empty gym.

We are contemplating where to breakfast when Pete pulls up, parks, and gets out with three coffees and a box of doughnuts.

"Closers get doughnuts," he says.

"Closers will take them," Blade says.

He hands us our coffees.

"Thank you," I say.

We stroll over to McKenzie Park and sit on a bench beneath a pair of enormous and ancient oak trees.

Pete opens the box, withdraws a doughnut, and passes the box to Blade. After she withdraws two, she passes it to me.

The doughnuts are still warm, their sugary glaze clinging to my skin as they collapse a little beneath the pinch of my fingers.

"Y'all keep solvin' our cases we gonna have to put y'all on the payroll," Pete says.

"What'd Nate say at first appearance?" I ask.

"He plead guilty like he said he would. Told the judge he didn't mean to kill her."

I nod. "Good. Figured he'd change his mind overnight and plead not guilty."

"What'd the daughter say last night?" Pete asks.

"That she wishes she'd never hired us," Blade says.

"Another satisfied customer," he says. Turning back to me he asks, "Have you gotten an update on Lexi?"

I shake my head. "Family told me not to call back. Said I'd be hearing from their attorney."

"About what?"

"Getting her shot I think."

"Damn."

Blade says, "That's some cold shit right there."

The background track of our conversation is the desultory sounds of Massalina Bayou, the shrieks of gulls, the metallic clanging of sailboat rigging, and the opening and closing of the Tarpon Dock drawbridge letting boats enter and exit the small inlet.

The park is in a serene state of perfection this morning—empty, relatively quiet, and the cool bay breeze causes the branches above us to gently undulate, the Spanish moss-draped across them waving back and forth.

Pete says, "I hear you and Ashlynn are lookin' for a bigger place so y'all can move into together."

I nod.

"What would you think about getting an even bigger one and letting me move in too?"

"That'd be great."

"Shit," Blade says, "what y'all tryin' to do? Recreate the orphanage?"

"We could if you'd join us," I say.

"I already see your ass all day," she says. "Got to see you all night too?"

"Before I forget," Pete says, "John Jordan said to tell you the

Gulf County Sheriff's Office won't be bringing any charges against y'all."

"Seems like you could've led with that," I say.

"Sorry, I—"

Before he can finish, Clyde Broussard walks up.

"Sorry to interrupt," he says.

"No problem," I say, then hold the box out to him. "Doughnut?"

He holds up his giant hand and shakes his head. "No, thank you. I'm here on business."

"What's up?"

"Destiny is missing," he says.

Blade says, "She finally wised up and did a runner."

"More likely Owens did something to her," I say.

Broussard says, "He's the one asking you to find her."

"Asking?" I say.

"Well . . ."

Blade says, "She really missin'?"

He nods. "He had me look for her first. I was as thorough as I knew how to be. Think somebody grabbed her."

"Creep from the club?" she says.

He shrugs. "I'm not a detective, but . . . I haven't been able to come up with anything."

"Wherever she is," Blade says, "whoever she's with . . . probably better than Owens."

Broussard looks at me. "Owens told me to tell you that if you find her he'll give you the blackmail video and your business with him will be done."

"Then it looks like we've got our next case," I say.

"Yeah," Blade says, "Stripper in a haystack."

SERIES SALE

For a limited time the entire John Jordan series is on sale!

CLICK HERE to complete your series for the best price EVER!

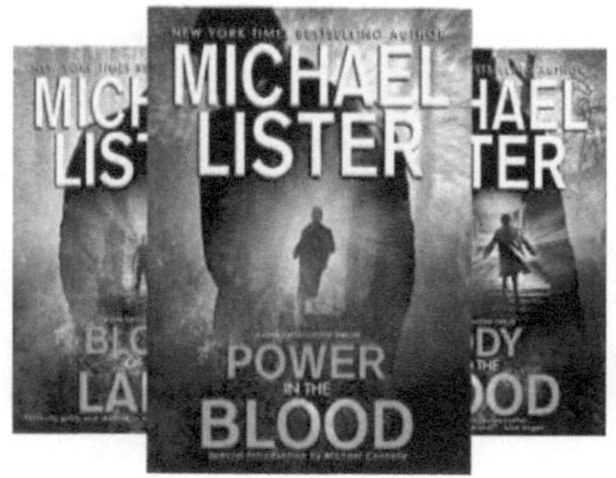

ALSO BY MICHAEL LISTER

(John Jordan Novels)

Power in the Blood

Blood of the Lamb

The Body and the Blood

Double Exposure

Blood Sacrifice

Rivers to Blood

Burnt Offerings

Innocent Blood

(Special Introduction by Michael Connelly)

Separation Anxiety

Blood Money

Blood Moon

Thunder Beach

Blood Cries

A Certain Retribution

Blood Oath

Blood Work

Cold Blood

Blood Betrayal

Blood Shot

Blood Ties

Blood Stone

Blood Trail

Bloodshed

Blue Blood

And the Sea Became Blood

The Blood-Dimmed Tide

Blood and Sand

A John Jordan Christmas

Blood Lure

Blood Pathogen

Beneath a Blood-Red Sky

Out for Blood

What Child is This?

Blood Reckoning

(Burke and Blade Mystery Thrillers)

The Night Of

The Night in Question

All Night Long

Dark of Night

Dead of Night

(Jimmy Riley Novels)

The Girl Who Said Goodbye

The Girl in the Grave

The Girl at the End of the Long Dark Night

The Girl Who Cried Blood Tears

The Girl Who Blew Up the World

(Merrick McKnight / Reggie Summers Novels)

Thunder Beach

A Certain Retribution

Blood Oath

Blood Shot

(Remington James Novels)

Double Exposure

(includes intro by Michael Connelly)

Separation Anxiety

Blood Shot

(Sam Michaels / Daniel Davis Novels)

Burnt Offerings

Blood Oath

Cold Blood

Blood Shot

(Love Stories)

Carrie's Gift

(Short Story Collections)

North Florida Noir

Florida Heat Wave

Delta Blues

Another Quiet Night in Desperation

(The Meaning Series)

Meaning Every Moment

The Meaning of Life in Movies

Sign up for Michael's newsletter by clicking here or go to

www.MichaelLister.com and receive a free book.

www.ingramcontent.com/pod-product-compliance
Lightning Source LLC
Chambersburg PA
CBHW030520310726
48979CB00010B/1746/J
9781947606975